80 002 955 874

Terence Blacker writes fiction for both children
and adults. The bestselling *Ms Wiz* books were
first published in 1989 and have been translat-
ed into fifteen languages so far. His novels for
older children include *The Transfer*, *The Angel
Factory*, *Boy2Girl* and *ParentSwap*. When he is
not writing he likes to play the guitar, write
songs and score goals for his football team.

What the reviewers have said about *Ms Wiz*:

"Hilarious and hysterical"
Susan Hill, *Sunday Times*

"Terence Blacker has created
a splendid character in the magical
Ms Wiz. Enormous fun"
Scotsn

"Sparkling zany hun
funn
Children's Books of the Year

You're Kidding, Ms Wiz

Ms Wiz Smells a Rat

Ms Wiz and the Sister of Doom

The Secret Life of Ms Wiz

Terence Blacker

Illustrated by Tony Ross

MACMILLAN CHILDREN'S BOOKS

Northamptonshire Libraries & Information Service	
80 002 955 874	
Peters	22-May-2009
CF	£4.99

This omnibus edition published 2006 by Macmillan Children's Books
a division of Macmillan Publishers Limited
20 New Wharf Road, London N1 9RR
Basingstoke and Oxford
www.panmacmillan.com

Associated companies throughout the world

ISBN-13: 978-0-330-44287-9
ISBN-10: 0-330-44287-2

Text copyright © Terence Blacker 1996, 1998, 1999, 2002 and 2006
Illustrations copyright © Tony Ross 1996, 1998, 1999, 2002 and 2006

The right of Terence Blacker and Tony Ross to be identified as the
author and illustrator of this work has been asserted by them in
accordance with the Copyright, Designs and Patents Act 1988.

All rights reserved. No part of this publication may be
reproduced, stored in or introduced into a retrieval system, or
transmitted, in any form or by any means (electronic, mechanical,
photocopying, recording or otherwise), without the prior written
permission of the publisher. Any person who does any unauthorized
act in relation to this publication may be liable to criminal
prosecution and civil claims for damages.

3 5 7 9 8 6 4 2

A CIP catalogue record for this book is available from
the British Library.

Typeset by Intype Libra Ltd
Printed and bound in Great Britain by Mackays of Chatham plc, Kent

This book is sold subject to the condition that it shall not,
by way of trade or otherwise, be lent, resold, hired out,
or otherwise circulated without the publisher's prior consent
in any form of binding or cover other than that in which
it is published and without a similar condition including this
condition being imposed on the subsequent purchaser.

You're Kidding,
Ms Wiz

*This book is dedicated to the children
of The Cedars Primary School,
Cranford, Middlesex*

CHAPTER ONE

A Very Regrettable Announcement

All day long, a tall, dark-suited stranger had been seen around the classrooms and corridors of St Barnabas School.

He had wandered in and out of the staff room, a weird, distant smile on his face. At lunch, he had sat in the dining room with the head teacher Mr Gilbert and had picked at his food, nodding seriously as the older man spoke.

He was sitting at the back of Miss Gomaz's classroom as Class Five arrived for their afternoon lesson. When Caroline Smith and Lizzie Thompson smiled at him, he made a note on the pad in front of him. Then Jack Beddows, who had always been something of a big mouth, asked him if he was a school inspector.

For a moment, the stranger had stared back with grey, unblinking eyes. "Not exactly," he said.

"Who *is* that weirdo?" muttered Jack as he sat beside his best friend Podge Harris.

"He's like The Thing From Outer Space," said Podge.

Miss Gomaz walked in. Somehow, she seemed paler than usual and ignored the man in the suit sitting at the back of her classroom.

"We shall be ending today's lesson ten minutes early," she said. "Mr Gilbert has an announcement to make to the whole school."

An announcement? At the end of the school day rather than at Assembly? The children of Class Five looked at one another. It was all very strange.

And it was just about to get even stranger.

*

"Ahem." Mr Gilbert stood before the entire school in the school hall. Although he was a small man, he usually had a sort of bouncy authority to him. But today he looked shrivelled, dusty and old. Standing nearby, the tall, dark-suited stranger seemed to tower over him.

"Ah, well, I expect you're all wondering why I have asked you to gather here today." Mr Gilbert gave a sort of wince. "It's because I have a very important, very regrettable announcement." He hesitated, then took a deep breath. "This morning each of your parents will have received a letter. It tells them—" With a sudden movement, the head teacher reached into his pocket for a handkerchief and blew his nose loudly. When he looked up, his glasses were misted. "It tells them that, at the end of this summer term, St Barnabas School is to close."

There was a gasp from the children in the hall, followed by a confusion of whispered voices.

"But why?" asked Caroline, who was sitting with the rest of Class Five, leaning against the wall to Mr Gilbert's right.

"Why?" The head teacher gave a long and heartfelt sigh. Briefly he seemed to have forgotten what he was going to say, until the tall stranger standing nearby cleared his throat. Mr Gilbert glanced in his direction. "Perhaps I could ask Mr Andrews, the local Education Officer, to explain to you the reasons why St Barnabas has to close."

The Education Officer stepped forward. He clasped his hands in front of him, looked down at the children, then suddenly bared his teeth like a man who has been taking lessons on how to smile but hasn't quite got the hang of it yet. "It is of course a matter of the deepest regret when any educational establishment is forced to close," he intoned.

"Yeah, he looked really upset," muttered Lizzie.

The Education Officer glanced irritably down at Class Five. "Not that I see this as really a closure. It's more an extension of parents' choice to use another school."

"What's he talking about?" said Caroline.

Again the Education Officer paused and stared threateningly at the row of Class Five children before turning back to his audience again. "Which is why a decision has been made, after much heart-searching."

"He'd have to search to find his heart," said Jack.

"So, as from next term" – the Education Officer raised his voice – "the pupils of this school will be absorbed into that of your good friends and neighbours, Brackenhurst Primary School."

"*Brackenhurst*, eurgh!" Podge spoke loudly as if he had just trodden in something disgusting.

"We will, of course, be prepared to listen to your parents' views but I have to say that it would take something very exceptional to make us change our minds."

Podge nudged Jack. "Very exceptional," he whispered. "Maybe this is a case for Ms Wiz."

"Yes!" Several of the children of Class Five picked up Podge's words. The whisper went down the row: "Ms Wiz, it's a case for Ms Wiz, we're going to find Ms Wiz."

The Education Officer had stopped talking and was staring down at Podge.

"Perhaps we could all share this private conversation of yours," he said nastily. "Who or what is wiz?"

"Ah, yes, wiz, er . . . " Podge hesitated, then smiled suddenly. "I was just saying . . . I'm really desperate to go for a wiz," he said.

The Education Officer sighed. "A wiz? What's a . . .? Oh, I see. Yes, all right then."

Winking at Jack, Podge stood up and made his way out of the hall.

Outside, the school was deserted. Podge walked down the corridor and into his classroom. There he sat gloomily at his desk and buried his face in his hands. "Absorbed into Brackenhurst," he moaned. "I don't believe it."

"Bad show, eh?"

Podge looked up. There, sitting on Miss Gomaz's desk, was a rat. It smiled at him. "Yes, old boy, it's me," it said.

Podge had only met one talking, smiling rat in his life. Its name was Herbert and it belonged to Ms Wiz.

8

"Herbert?" said Podge.

"At your service, old bean," said
the rat.

"Good old Ms Wiz." Podge
laughed with relief. "She always said
she went where magic was needed.
We thought she had left the area –
we haven't seen her for two years. She
must have heard that St Barnabas
was in trouble so she sent you along
to find out what was—"

"You're joking." Herbert gave a

ratty little laugh. "There is no Ms Wiz these days. She's Mrs Dolores Arnold."

"You mean . . .?"

"Yup. Married," said Herbert. "Married alive. And worst of all—"

At that moment, the sound of children's voices could be heard coming down the corridor.

"Quick," said Podge, grabbing Herbert and putting him inside his jacket pocket.

The door was flung open. "So that's it," said Jack, who was followed by the rest of Class Five. "The best school in the world and they're going to close it down."

"Maybe," said Podge. "And maybe not."

CHAPTER TWO

Dunwizzin

Very few people stared at Podge and Jack as they walked down the High Street after school, which was odd, since Podge was carrying Herbert the rat on his right shoulder.

"I suppose people like to mind their own business," said Jack when Podge pointed this out.

"Either that or they don't want a nipped finger," said Herbert. "I can't stand it when people treat me like some kind of pet. Next street on the left, old bean."

They turned into a narrow, tree-lined street at the end of which, between two larger houses, they saw a tiny cottage almost obscured by roses and ivy. Podge looked at the wooden sign on the garden gate.

"Dunwizzin," he read. "That's a funny name for a house. I wonder what it means."

"When people retire, they call their houses 'Dunroamin'," said Jack. "Ms Wiz must be telling the world that she's retired from magic." He strode up the short garden path and rang the doorbell. "We'll soon see about that," he said.

From inside the cottage came the sound of approaching footsteps. The door was flung open.

"Hi!"

The woman who stood on the doorstep had the long, dark hair of Ms Wiz. She had the slightly surprised look that Ms Wiz used to have. The silver moons which dangled from her ears were exactly the sort of thing which Ms Wiz would once have worn. And yet there was something strangely different about her.

"Er, Ms Wiz?" said Jack nervously.

"Jack!" The woman laughed with pleasure. "Of course it's me." Before Jack could move away, she leant down to kiss his cheek. "Mwa," she said loudly.

Jack stepped back and rubbed his cheek.

"See what I mean?" murmured Herbert to Podge. "She's gone all normal on us."

"Podge!" Ms Wiz was just about to kiss Podge when she saw Herbert on his shoulder. "And there you are, you naughty rat," she said.

"Just don't kiss me, right?" said Herbert.

"Mwa!" Avoiding Herbert, Ms Wiz kissed Podge, then turned back into the cottage. "Come in, come in," she said. "What a gorgeous surprise this is."

"Yeah, gorgeous," said Podge. Glancing at Jack, he followed Ms Wiz into the house.

"I'm afraid it's all a bit of a mess in here," Ms Wiz was saying as she led them through a little hall and into the kitchen. "We've just finished decorating downstairs. D'you like the spring lilac look we've gone for? And what about these adorable fitted units?"

The children stared in amazement.

"Are you feeling all right, Ms Wiz?" asked Podge.

"Yes, of course I am," said Ms Wiz. "Why d'you ask?"

Jack lifted Herbert off Podge's shoulders and put him on the floor. "All this kissing and stuff about gorgeous, adorable, lilac kitchen units – it doesn't seem like you somehow. You've become so . . . homey."

"Ah yes, there's no place like home," smiled Ms Wiz.

"Whatever happened to all the magic?" asked Jack. "You used to be happy going around in a beaten-up old car that used to hover in the air and change into—"

"There's a different kind of magic these days," Ms Wiz said quickly. "The magic of being Mrs Brian Arnold. He'll be home soon."

"So that's all you do these days?" Podge asked. "Hang around your gorgeous, adorable kitchen waiting for your husband to come home? Boy, you've changed."

"Actually," Ms Wiz smiled as she opened a drawer in the kitchen table and took out an exercise book, "I've got a new job."

She handed the book to Podge. "I'm going to be a writer – tell the story of my life. It's going to be a best-seller."

Podge read out the words on the front of the exercise book. *"There's No Business Like Ms Wizness – The Memoirs of a Paranormal Operative."*

"Exciting, eh?" said Ms Wiz.

"Yeah, great," muttered Podge. "So instead of doing magic, you'll be writing about it."

"Exactly," said Ms Wiz. "I know I'm going to *love* writing."

"It's a real shame that you've gone into retirement," said Jack. "We needed a bit of magic after the surprise we were given today."

"Surprise." Ms Wiz held up a finger. "That reminds me. I have a small surprise for you."

She walked out of the kitchen and ran up the stairs.

"She's not listening," said Podge. "She was never exactly good at concentrating but she's all over the place these days."

"Yeah, it's just me, me, me," said Jack.

"And here's my surprise." Ms Wiz stood at the kitchen door. There was a small bundle of white clothes in her arms.

"I don't believe it," said Jack.

"A *baby*?" said Podge.

"Say hello to William," said Ms Wiz. "Otherwise known as the Wiz Kid."

Neither Jack nor Podge had ever had a baby brother or sister in their families. For a few moments, as they looked at William, they behaved in the sort of way they had seen people behaving when a baby was around. They tickled its tummy. They tweaked its tiny toes. They made goo-goo noises.

"Now who wants to hold William?" asked Ms Wiz eventually.

The boys looked at one another.

"Er, no, Ms Wiz," said Podge. "I'm not exactly a baby person, to tell the truth."

"Nor me," said Jack quickly. "I might drop it."

"It? Don't be ridiculous." Ms Wiz gave the baby to Jack. "William's not a thing, you know."

Jack looked down at the tiny figure in his arms as Ms Wiz went to put the kettle on. "Hey, cool baby," he said. William smiled up at him.

"Let's have a go," said Podge, reaching for him.

"Get off," said Jack, holding the baby more tightly. "You can have him in a minute."

"Easy, guys."

Jack and Podge looked at one another, then down at the baby. The tiny voice had seemed to come from the Wiz Kid himself.

"You heard what the lady said – I'm not a thing." William winked deliberately.

"Ms Wiz." Jack frowned. "I think you've got a magic baby here."

"Oh thank you, Jack," said Ms Wiz.

"No, I meant a *magic* magic baby."

"He'll have to be changed soon," said Ms Wiz.

"Changed? Into what?" asked Podge.

Ms Wiz smiled. "His nappies." She took the Wiz Kid and carefully put him in a cot near the window. "Not everything has to be weird and wonderful, you know."

"No," said Podge. "Of course not."

"So you never told me what your surprise was," said Ms Wiz.

"Ah yes, our surprise," said Jack. "Well, yesterday we had a visit from this weirdo hairdo from outer space."

"Weirdo hairdo?"

"He turned out to be an Education Officer." Sitting on the side of the kitchen table, Jack explained everything that had happened that day – how St Barnabas was

21

going to be merged with Brackenhurst.

"*Brackenhurst?*" Ms Wiz looked
shocked.

"Exactly," said Jack. "So we badly
need your help."

"Hmm." Ms Wiz paced
backwards and forwards, deep in
thought. "I suppose I could write
some letters," she said eventually.
"Say what a wonderful school St
Barnabas is."

"That's just words, Ms Wiz," said Podge. "We meant something a bit paranormal."

"Paranormal?" Ms Wiz sighed. "I'm not sure about that. When I married Brian, I promised that I wouldn't get involved in magic again."

"But Ms Wiz," Jack pleaded.

Ms Wiz held up both hands. "A promise is a promise," she said.

"There's a parents' meeting at

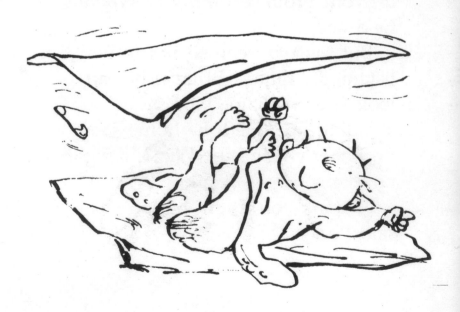

Podge's house tomorrow," said Jack. "Maybe you could come along as a future parent. What d'you think, Podge?"

Podge seemed to be staring in the direction of the Wiz Kid. A bright white nappy was hovering over the cot and a faint humming sound could be heard from the far side of the kitchen.

"Hm?" Podge returned his attention to the discussion. "Ms Wiz, do your promises apply to William?" he asked.

But Ms Wiz seemed not to be listening. "I'll ask Brian if he can look after William," she said, standing up. "He'll be home soon. I'd better change the Wiz Kid right now."

"I think you might be too late," said Podge.

CHAPTER THREE

No More Magic?

Ms Wiz walked slowly back to the kitchen.

"Normal or paranormal?" she murmured to herself. "Wife or weirdo?"

"Wife *and* weirdo."

Ms Wiz looked down to see Herbert the rat on one of the kitchen chairs.

"Just because you got married, you don't need to change who you are," he said. "To the outside world, you may be Mrs Arnold, but underneath you're still Ms Wiz, paranormal operative."

"Excuse me, Herbert," said Ms Wiz. "I think I can do without a lecture from a rat, thank you very much."

"Think of St Barnabas. All your
friends there. Podge, Caroline, Jack,
Lizzie, poor shy little Nabila—"

"But you know how Brian hates
magic," Ms Wiz sighed. "He thinks
it isn't natural to have a wife who
can fly and cast spells and talk to
her rat."

"*So* old-fashioned," said Herbert.
"Oh well, if you're happy to be the
little wifey—"

"Enough!" Ms Wiz slapped the

kitchen table with the palm of her hand. "I've told you before that if you don't behave like a normal rat, I'll take you down to the pet shop."

"Normal," grumbled Herbert as he wandered off to the doll's house in the corner where he lived. "Suddenly everything has to be normal."

"Yes, it does." Ms Wiz picked up her exercise book. "Anyway I'm not going to be a little wifey. I'm going to be a best-selling author and let the magic come through in my books."

"Dream on, Dol."

The voice came from the other side of the kitchen where William was leaning over the side of his pram. "Those kids need real magic to save their school, not book magic."

Ms Wiz groaned. "This place is becoming a madhouse," she said. "And I've told you not to call me Dol. If you have to talk to me, at least call me Mummy like other babies do."

"Sure, Dol," said the Wiz Kid.

"I am not going to sit here in my own kitchen being bullied by my baby and my rat," said Ms Wiz firmly. She opened the door into the garden and pushed the pram into the shade of a tree.

"You have an afternoon sleep, while I do some writing."

"You didn't mind me using magic to change my nappies," mumbled the Wiz Kid.

"That's different." Ms Wiz kissed William, then walked back into the kitchen, where she sat at the table. Picking up the exercise book, she turned to the first page and started to read.

Once upon a time I was a paranormal operative. Hardly a day would pass when I didn't do something really rather magical. Sometimes I flew around on a vacuum cleaner. Other

days, I turned teachers into geese or travelled back in time or became Prime Minister for the afternoon. On one occasion, I even used my magic FISH powder to bring characters from books to life.

But that was then and this is now. For the past two years, I have been plain Mrs Dolores Arnold, wife of Brian, mother of William, a happy, ordinary, unmagical person. My family and my lovely home are enough for *me. There's no more need for spells or magic.*

With a weary smile, Ms Wiz laid the exercise book on the table. The trouble was, she thought to herself, she *did* need spells and magic. Spells could be used to keep St Barnabas open. Magic would help bring her book to life. It seemed to her that, however hard she tried, her adventures were never quite as exciting written down as they had been in real life.

"FISH powder," she said to herself thoughtfully. FISH had stood for Freeing Illustrated Storybook Heroes. "I wonder if it would bring my book to life as well." She shook her head. "No, a promise is a promise."

Yet, slowly, as if in a trance, she walked to the kitchen cupboard, murmuring quietly to herself. "On the other hand, maybe a little private magic, just between me and my book, wouldn't make any difference." She took out a small bottle marked "FISH Powder" and carefully sprinkled it over every page of her exercise book.

She had just finished when the door opened.

"Hi, Dolores, I'm home." Brian Arnold stood at the kitchen door. He was tall and dark-haired and wore spectacles which gave him a serious, owlish, tired look.

"Hi, Brian." Ms Wiz kissed her husband.

"Busy day?"

"Quite busy," said Ms Wiz. "Some of my old friends from St Barnabas came round. Apparently there's a plan to close the school."

"Oh dear," said Brian casually. "Where's William?"

"In the garden," said Ms Wiz. "Getting his energy up for staying awake all night."

"Hmm." Casually Brian Arnold picked up Ms Wiz's exercise book and glanced at the pages.

A faint humming noise filled the kitchen. Before Ms Wiz's eyes, a sort of cloud enveloped Brian. When it cleared, an astonishing sight greeted her eyes.

"No more magic, eh?" Herbert laughed quietly from the corner.

"I don't believe it," said Ms Wiz. "So *that's* what the FISH powder does."

CHAPTER FOUR

Such Charming Children

Podge, Lizzie, Jack and Caroline were
sitting in a corner in Podge's sitting
room, watching as their parents
worked on an action plan to save St
Barnabas. They had been talking for
half an hour. So far there had been
no plan and the only action had
been when Mr Harris, Podge's
father, had spilt his tea while waving
his arms about as he made a point.

"All I'm saying is that we've got to
work through the right channels," said
Mr Harris. "Now it just so happens
that I have a few friends in high
places on the council. Say the word,
I'll pull a few strings – then I'll pass a
motion on the education committee."

"Oh Cuthbert," sighed Mrs Harris.
"You and your motions."

Mrs Thompson, Lizzie's mother, raised a hand nervously. "Surely we need to get a petition together. Lots and lots of signatures."

"Pop stars," said Jack's father, Mr Beddows, suddenly. "Pop stars are always supporting lost causes."

"How about a party?" suggested Mrs Smith, Caroline's mum. "We could all organize a terrific, huge fund-raising wingding."

"Typical," grumbled Mr Smith,

who was sitting beside her. "Trust my wife to think up another excuse for a party."

"At least I thought of something," snapped Mrs Smith. "The only thing you ever think of is going down to the pub."

"Through the chair, through the chair, *please*." Mr Harris banged the table in front of him. "I call the meeting to order. All those in favour of my passing a motion say Aye."

More voices joined in.

"Who said he was the chairman?"

"What about my party idea?"

"Does anyone know any pop stars?"

The parents were making so much noise that no one except Podge heard the doorbell ring. They were so busy talking that, for several seconds, none of them noticed that someone else had arrived at the meeting and now stood at the door to the sitting room.

"Hullo, who's this?" said Mr Harris at last.

"It's Mrs Arnold," Podge said. "She's come to the meeting as a St Barnabas parent of the future."

"That's no Mrs Arnold," Mrs Thompson laughed. "That's Ms Wiz. I'd recognize her anywhere."

"Wiz? That witch woman?" Mr Harris frowned and folded his arms. "I'll have nothing to do with any paranormal hanky-panky. I'm a respectable man."

"And I'm a respectable woman," said Ms Wiz, smiling. "In fact, I'm a mum – and you can't get much more respectable than that."

"Ms Wiz got married and the magic faded," Jack explained.

"I know the feeling," murmured Mrs Smith, glancing at her husband.

"How old is your baby?" asked Mrs Thompson.

Ms Wiz smiled. "He's almost a year – but he's quite advanced for his age."

"You can say that again," muttered Podge.

"I was wondering whether there was going to be a Beautiful Baby Contest at the school fête?" Ms Wiz asked.

"There always is," said Mrs Thompson. "But what's that got to do with saving St Barnabas?"

"I think I'll enter William," said Ms Wiz firmly. "And will there be a book stall?"

"I'm looking after that," said Mrs Beddows. "Any old volumes are welcome."

"What about a new volume?" asked Ms Wiz. She reached into the bag hanging over her shoulder and took out her purple exercise book.

As she opened the book, Jack nudged Podge. "She's wearing black nail varnish," he whispered. "You know what that means."

Ms Wiz held the book open in front of the parents. "I was wondering if there would be a market for my memoirs," she said.

"Black nail varnish," said Podge quietly. "Maybe the magic hasn't faded."

As if in reply, a strange humming noise could be heard and a thick mist filled the room.

"Books and babies," Mr Harris was muttering. "I've never heard anything so ... *I want my mummy!*"

As the mist cleared, an extra-ordinary sight was revealed. In the place of the seven parents stood seven children. Amongst them, a small, fat boy was crying. The rest were looking around, confused.

"Eh?" Jack stared in amazement. "What's going on?"

"Just an experiment, Jack." Ms Wiz smiled. "I told you my writing was magical."

"But who are these people?" asked Podge.

"They're your parents," said Ms Wiz. "When I put some magic powder on the pages, my book seems to take its readers back to their childhood."

"I want my mummy!" Mr Harris's small, round face had turned the colour of a tomato.

"He's rather sweet, your dad," Jack
said to Podge.

Podge shook his head in disbelief.
"He's even fatter than I am," he said.
"And he always told me he was thin
when he was a child."

"He certainly seems to have
forgotten about his motion," said Ms
Wiz.

"Look at my parents," whispered
Caroline. "They're holding hands.
I've never seen them do that before."

Mr Harris had turned to Podge. "Have *you* seen my mummy?" he sniffed miserably.

"Granny? I mean, your mum? Er, not since last Christmas, no," said Podge.

Tears welled up once more in Mr Harris's eyes.

"Ms Wiz, this is getting too weird for me," said Podge. "I can't get used to being four years older than my father."

"Jolly interesting." Ms Wiz sat on a chair nearby to watch.

"Such charming children." She sighed. "And then they grew up."

"But these aren't really children," said Caroline with a hint of panic in her voice. "Could we have our parents back now, please?"

"Honestly," sighed Ms Wiz. "First you want magic, then you don't." She took the bottle of FISH powder from her pocket, stood up and sprinkled it over the seven children. "REDWOP HSIF! REDWOP HSIF!" she muttered.

As the loud humming noise returned, the room was once again obscured by a heavy mist.

" . . . it's all a load of nonsense is what I say." Podge's dad, as large and as adult as he had ever been, stood among the parents.

Mr and Mrs Smith were staring at one another in amazement. They were still holding hands. Slowly they both smiled.

"I mean, a bloomin' book's not going to change anything, is it?" said Mr Harris, turning to the four children. "What are you lot staring at?" he asked.

"He was such a shy little boy, your dad," said Jack. "I wonder what changed him."

"I'll tell you this, my lad. When I was a young 'un, I kept my mouth

shut and minded my own business,"
said Mr Harris.

"Yeah, Dad," said Podge. "Of
course you did."

Ms Wiz picked up her exercise
book and slipped it back into her
shoulder bag. "A very successful
experiment, I think," she said
quietly. "Now for the school fête."

CHAPTER FIVE

Shazam

Apart from the big banner reading
"SOS! SAVE OUR SCHOOL", which
had been draped over the wire
surrounding the playground, the St
Barnabas School fête was much like
any other.

On a platform that had been
erected in front of the school, Mr
Gilbert was making announcements
into a microphone. The Lady
Mayoress, who had opened the fête,
stood nearby, looking large and
regal. In the background, the iron-
grey head of the Education Officer
could be seen bobbing about with
nervous self-importance.

"Where *is* she?" said Jack, who was
standing with Podge beside Mrs
Thompson's cake stall.

"Mm?" Podge took a bite of the bun in his hand and began chewing slowly.

"Ms Wiz promised to be here," said Jack, scanning the playground with his eyes.

Podge swallowed. "Probably that husband of hers," he said. "It didn't sound as if he was too happy about Ms Wiz coming out of retirement." He took another bite of the bun.

Looking at him, Jack shook his head. "Gross," he muttered.

"It'sh shtreshh," protested Podge, spraying Jack with crumbs. "When I'm stressed, I have to eat," he said. "And I get particularly stressed if one of Mrs Thompson's buns is near me."

"Make way, make way!" At that moment, there was a commotion from the gates to the playground. Wearing a bright orange trouser suit, Ms Wiz could be seen carving her

way through the crowd, a pram in front of her.

"Over here, Ms Wiz," shouted Jack.

"Phew, I knew we should have flown. The traffic was terrible." Ms Wiz pushed her hair out of her eyes. "Brian's coming along later."

Podge looked into the pram. "All right, Will?" he said.

The Wiz Kid lifted his tiny thumb and winked.

"Last call for the Beautiful Baby

Contest," Mr Gilbert was saying.

"All right." Ms Wiz looked around her and dropped her voice. "Here's the plan." She reached under the blanket in the pram, took out her purple exercise book and handed it to Jack. "You give my book to the Education Officer. He reads it and – shazam!"

"Shazam?" said Jack.

"He'll be putty in your hands once he's a child," Ms Wiz smiled. "Children always do what they're told."

"I can tell you haven't been a mum for long," said Podge.

"But where will you be?" asked Jack.

"We'll be winning the Beautiful Baby Contest."

"Yeah!" A tiny voice could be heard from the pram. "Going for gold!"

"Oh, and you'll need this." Ms Wiz

reached into her pocket and took out a small bottle. "When you want to undo the spell, just sprinkle some powder over the Education Officer and say "FISH POWDER" backwards – that's 'HSIF REDWOP'."

"HSIF REDWOP," said Jack carefully trying to remember the spell.

"But this is crazy, Ms Wiz," said Podge desperately. "You're meant to be the Paranormal Operative round here, not us."

Ms Wiz shrugged helplessly. "A promise is a promise," she said, turning the pram towards where the other mothers and babies were gathering.

"Thanks for nothing, Ms Wiz," Podge muttered as they watched her walk away. "So how are we going to get the Education Officer to change his mind?"

Jack was tapping the tip of his nose, a sure sign that a cunning idea

was occurring to him. "A promise is
a promise," he said quietly. "OK,
Podge. Here's what we do..."

Moments later, they were walking
over to the platform where the
Education Officer was seated next to
Mr Gilbert.

"Peter, Jack." The head teacher
smiled down at them. "How are you
enjoying the fête?"

"Very much," said Jack. "We have
a present for the Education Officer."

"A present?" The Education Officer turned slowly to them.

"Class Five wanted to apologize for interrupting your announcement last week," said Podge in his most angelic voice.

The Education Officer turned to Mr Gilbert. "Maybe you were right about this class of yours," he murmured. "Sometimes they seem almost human."

Mr Gilbert narrowed his eyes suspiciously. "I'll believe it when I see it," he said.

"So where is this present of mine?" asked the Education Officer.

"In the classroom, sir," said Jack with an innocent smile. "Would you like us to take you there?"

Looking slightly embarrassed, the Education Officer followed Jack and Podge into the school building, along the corridor and into Class Five's classroom. While Podge closed the door behind them, Jack slipped the purple exercise book on to one of the desks.

"Ah, here it is, sir," he said, picking it up again and handing it to the Education Officer.

"This is our class project," said Podge. "It's all about things that happened to us when we were in Class Three. We called it *There's No Business Like Ms Wizness*."

"What a funny title."

"That's explained inside, sir," said Jack. "Maybe you'd like to read it."

The Education Officer opened the purple exercise book and stared at the first page. Within seconds, the classroom was filled with the sound of a humming noise and a thick, choking mist.

When the mist cleared, the Education Officer was nowhere to be seen. In his place stood a small boy with neatly parted hair.

"Hello," he said, with a shy smile. "My name is Laurence Andrews. My friends call me Larry."

"Hi, Larry," said Jack.

"Have we met?" asked the little boy.

"Er, not exactly," said Podge.

Jack sat down at one of the desks and let out a long, heartfelt sigh. "We have got *such* a problem, Larry," he said miserably. "A horrid man has just told us that our school is going to be closed down."

"Oh dear," said Larry.

Podge slumped down tragically at the next-door desk. "We're all going to be sent away to another school, full of lots of big boys and girls who are real bullies," he sniffed.

"Oh dear oh dear," said Larry, the corners of his mouth turning down, his chin trembling.

"Our teachers will all be fired and the buildings torn down," said Jack quietly. "All gone . . . our games, our friendships, our special football team." He stared out of the window. "And we were all *so* happy here too."

Tears had filled Larry's eyes. "Stop it, stop it, I can't stand it," he sobbed. "If only there were something I could do."

Podge shook his head. "The only thing you can do is promise that, when you grow up, you'll never have anything to do with closing down a nice school like this one."

"Close a school down?" Larry looked shocked. "Why on earth would I want to do that?"

"Just promise, please," said Jack.

"All right, all right, I promise," said Larry. "That's the one thing I'll never ever do."

"Thanks, Larry." Jack stood up, the bottle of FISH powder in his hand.

He sprinkled some on the little boy's neat hair. "FISH FLIP FLOP," he said.

Nothing happened.

"Er, HASIF REDMOP?" tried Jack.

"Excuse me, but what are you doing?" asked Larry.

"It's HSIF REDWOP," said Podge, "HSIF—" And, before he had finished, the classroom was once again filled with a dense mist.

As it cleared, the Education Officer stood where Larry had been seconds before. "Now where were we?" He wiped his eyes and found to his surprise that the back of his hand appeared to be damp with tears.

"We were explaining what a special school St Barnabas is," said Jack. "All our friends . . . We are all so happy here."

The Education Officer frowned as if some distant memory was coming back to him.

"And that you seem to us the sort of person who would never have anything to do with closing down a nice school like this one," said Podge. "That was the one thing you would never ever do."

The Education Officer blinked and looked around him as if seeing the classroom for the first time. Then he stared out into the playground, thronging with happy children, parents and teachers. "I once made a promise," he whispered.

"A promise is . . . a promise," said Jack.

"You're right." Tucking Ms Wiz's purple exercise book under his arm, the Education Officer walked slowly to the door. "A promise *is* a promise. Maybe it's not too late."

"Go for it, Larry," smiled Jack.

The Education Officer hesitated at the door. "Larry? No one's called me that since I was at school."

"Cool name," said Podge.

"Thank you." The Education Officer left the room, shaking his head as if something very odd had happened to him.

Through the window, Jack and Podge watched as the Education Officer walked to the platform and picked up the microphone. "I have an announcement to make," he said. "It's about St Barnabas School . . . "

Seconds later, a great cheer echoed around the playground.

Sprinting across the playground, Jack and Podge found Ms Wiz and the Wiz Kid near the entrance.

"We did it!" shouted Podge.

"It worked!" Jack laughed, waving the bottle of FISH powder.

"Welcome to the world of magic." Ms Wiz smiled as she took the bottle and put it in her bag.

"Huh, *now* she likes magic," William muttered loudly from the pram.

"What happened in the Beautiful Baby contest?" asked Podge.

Ms Wiz sighed. "The Lady Mayoress looked into the pram and said, 'What a chubby little chap he is.' So William decided to reply."

"I only told her she was no bloomin' supermodel herself,"

grumbled William. "What was wrong with that?"

"Hi, Dolores." From behind them, Brian Arnold, Ms Wiz's husband, appeared. "Sorry I'm late. Did I miss anything?"

"You could say," said Jack.

"Not much," said Ms Wiz.

They were interrupted by Mrs Hicks making an announcement from the platform. "We have a lost child," she said, looking down at a small six-year-old in shorts who was standing beside her. "He says his name is Henry Gilbert."

"Sounds like you've got another reader," said Podge quietly. "That magical book of yours has just taken the head teacher back to his childhood."

"Magical book?" Mr Brian Arnold narrowed his eyes. "Have you been up to your tricks again?"

"Tricks? Not me." Ms Wiz reached into her bag and took out a small bottle of powder. She kissed her husband lightly on the cheek, then winked at Jack and Podge. "A writer's work is never done," she said.

Ms Wiz
Smells a Rat

For Jack Bardwell

Acknowledgement

I would like to thank Niall Bole of Holy Rosary Primary School, Belfast, for helping me with the title for this book.

CHAPTER ONE

An Early Morning Bite

It was early one summer's morning and Ms Wiz was in bed with her husband, Mr Arnold. They both had a busy day ahead of them – Mr Arnold was inspecting a school and Ms Wiz was trying to write the story of her life, *There's No Business Like Ms Wizness: The Memoirs of a Paranormal Operative*, as well as look after their baby William, who right now was sleeping in the next room.

But, just for a few moments, as the sun streamed through a gap in the curtains and the birds sang in the garden outside, they were relaxed.

"Heigh-ho." Mr Arnold reached for his spectacles on the bedside table. "Another lovely day."

Slowly, he pulled back the duvet and swung his legs out of bed. Sleepily, he felt for his slippers with his feet.

"AAAAGGGHHHH!"

Mr Arnold's scream shattered the peace of the morning. He leapt high in the air, his legs pedalling wildly. When he came down, he was standing on the bed, staring wide-eyed down at the floor.

"That bloomin', blinkin' . . . blastin' creature." With a shaking hand, Mr Arnold pointed downwards. "It bit me."

"Bit you?" Frowning, Ms Wiz peered over the edge of the bed, and smiled. "Oh, Herbert."

From the warm depths of Mr Arnold's slipper, a brown and white rat looked up, blinking. "Well, thank you very much," said Herbert the rat. "What a *lovely* wake-up call that was – a great big smelly foot coming down on me. *So* kind, I must say."

"I thought I asked you not to sleep in Brian's slipper." Ms Wiz tried to sound severe but somehow she was unable to keep the laughter out of her voice.

"I was lonely," said Herbert.

"And you know that you should never ever bite people."

"It wasn't a bite," said Herbert. "I was yawning and your husband decided to put his toe in my mouth." He gave a ratty shudder. "Not pleasant."

Mr Arnold sat down on the bed and turned his back deliberately on Herbert. "Dolores, I just cannot stand it any more." He spoke with the quiet dignity of a man about to make an important announcement. "Do you recall what I asked you on the day we got married?"

"You asked me to love and honour you until death do us—"

"*Apart* from that."

"Ah." Ms Wiz thought hard.

"Maybe . . . something about magic?" she said eventually.

"Precisely. We agreed that there would be no spells – that this house would be a magic-free zone. Now, what would you call a talking rodent who follows me about, eats my chocolate biscuits, complains about the TV programmes I like to watch and tells me I'm putting on weight every time I get in the bath? If that's not magic, what is?" Mr Arnold crossed his arms. "There are three of us in this marriage. It's getting a bit crowded."

"I'll ask him to behave," said Ms Wiz.

"Behave? That yellow-toothed, long-tailed hooligan? Forget it," said Mr Arnold. "I want him out."

"But Brian," said Ms Wiz. "He's been with me through thick and thin."

"And guess who the thick was," muttered Herbert.

Mr Arnold ignored him. "Either

that rat goes or I do," he said.

"Toodle-oo then," said Herbert. "Nice knowing you."

"Oh Herbert," murmured Ms Wiz sadly. "What am I going to do with you?

In the Harris household, Friday evenings were special. At seven o'clock Mr Harris would ring the local Italian takeaway and ask for three large pizzas to be delivered. At half past seven, the whole family – Mr Harris, Mrs Harris and their only son, Peter, who was known to his friends as Podge – would sit down to watch their favourite programme, *The Avenue*.

"This is what family life is all about," said Mr Harris, as they settled down with their pizzas that Friday night. "I've been working hard all week, you two have been messing around, doing whatever

you do. Now we can relax together – it's
lovely."

"Yes." Mrs Harris smiled. "We are a
lovely family, aren't we?"

"Family?" Mr Harris looked slightly
surprised. "I was talking about the
pizza. American Hot – my favourite."

It was at that moment that the front doorbell rang.

"Peter," said Mr Harris without taking his eyes off the television.

Podge put his pizza aside and made his way to the front door.

On the doorstep was a stooped figure in ragged clothes, a battered old cap on her head and a bright red scarf which hid most of her face. Over her arm, she carried a large basket.

"Apples, young man?" she croaked. "Very fresh, very cheap."

"No, thanks," said Podge.

"You won't regret it." The woman seemed to wink. "They've got a special ingredient added. It's called Herbert." She held out a paper bag and, for the first time, Podge noticed the black nail-varnish on her fingers.

"Ms Wiz?" he whispered.

Ms Wiz put a finger to her lips. "I need you to look after Herbert," she said

in a low voice. "Just for a bit."

"Herbert? But my dad hates—"

"What does your dad hate?" Behind
Podge, Mr Harris appeared in the hall,
his mouth greasy from pizza. "And
who's Herbert?"

Podge hesitated, thinking fast.

"Sherbet!" he said suddenly. "I was
just saying that you couldn't stand
sherbet." He grabbed the bag from Ms

Wiz. "No, we certainly don't want any sherbet apples in this house, thank you very much. But we'll take these." Clutching the paper bag, he closed the door quickly. "Sherbet apples," he said to his father. "What will they think of next?"

But Mr Harris was still staring at the door. "I'm sure I've seen that woman somewhere before."

CHAPTER TWO

A Bit Rattled

Moments later, Podge was closing the bedroom door behind him, carefully laying the paper bag on his bed. It crackled and moved for a moment. Then, with some difficulty, Herbert the rat squeezed himself between two apples and emerged into the light, blinking.

"Humans get huge lorries and vans when they move house," he grumbled. "What do I get? A paper bag full of old apples."

"Is that you, Herbert?" asked Podge.

Herbert sighed wearily. "Get a lot of talking rats round here, do you? Lots of intelligent rodents delivered in bags of apples by women wearing black nail-varnish and talking in a silly voice?"

"No need to be sarcastic," said Podge. "What was that you said about moving house?"

The rat sniffed. "Booted out of my very own home with not so much as a toothbrush."

"Toothbrush?" Podge glanced at Herbert's brownish teeth. "I never realized you used a—"

"Never mind, I'll share yours," said Herbert casually.

Podge gulped. "I don't want to sound rude," he said, quickly changing the subject. "But what exactly are you doing here?"

"Search me, old bean." Herbert the rat pointed his nose in the direction of the paper bag. "I believe there's some kind of note from Her Royal Ms Wizness."

Podge reached into the bag. Wedged between two apples was a piece of paper, the corner of which had been badly nibbled. Carefully, he unfolded the note and read it to himself.

Dear Podge

I've got a bit of a problem at home. You couldn't be a love and look after Herbert for while, could you? You were always his favourite at St Barnabas. He's no trouble but remember to leave a window open at night – he likes to wander about. I'll be in touch when I've sorted things out. Thanks a million.

Your old pal, Ms Wiz

PS I'm sorry about turning up disguised as an apple-seller. I promised Brian I wouldn't use any magic.

PPS Herbert likes the special fancy rat mixture you can get at pet shops.

PPPS And chocolate biscuits for a treat.

PPPPS He seems to be a bit grumpy at the moment – can't think why.

PPPPPS Give him a big kiss from me and tell him I'm missing him already.

"What did she say?" asked Herbert, trying to look casual and uninterested.

Podge hesitated. "She says she's missing you and she's asked me to give you a big kiss."

"Ugh, kiss a human?" Herbert leapt back. "You must be joking."

"I don't believe it." Podge stared at Ms Wiz's note, shaking his head.

"Oh, all right, I'll kiss you if it means so much to you," said Herbert.

"Eh? No, I meant this whole idea of you staying here. My parents can't stand animals. When I won a goldfish at a fair, I had to give it away because my mum didn't like the way it looked at her. My dad's idea of a good time is throwing stones at cats who come into the garden."

"Sensible man," said Herbert. "Nasty, unfriendly creatures, they are."

"But a rat in this house?" Podge groaned. "It's a nightmare."

"Not just any rat, old bean," said
Herbert. "I am a bit special."

"And that makes it worse," said
Podge. "Dad hates magic almost as
much as he hates animals."

Herbert sighed. "Well, you'll just have
to hide me," he said firmly. "A drawer
will do. With nice warm, woollen socks
– clean socks, if you don't mind."

From downstairs, Podge heard his
mother calling his name. "All right," he
sighed. "But I'd better go now. My pizza
will be getting cold."

"Mm, pizza, my favourite," said
Herbert.

He hopped towards Podge.

It was a particularly good episode of *The
Avenue* that night. There were two
arguments and a minor car crash, a
wedding was cancelled at the last minute
and someone got punched on the nose.

But Podge was too tense to enjoy it. Sitting on the edge of the sofa, eating his pizza, all he could think of was what had happened that evening.

Ms Wiz. The note. Herbert.

What would his dad say if he discovered that, not only had a talking rat come to stay, but at that very moment, it was hiding inside Podge's shirt?

"What's the matter, Peter?" his mother asked in a concerned tone of voice. "You're looking a bit peaky."

"Nothing," said Podge. "I just feel a bit . . . rattled this evening."

"Oh, very good joke," murmured Herbert from his hiding place.

"What was that?" said Mrs Harris.

"Must have been my stomach rumbling," said Podge quickly.

"I'm not surprised it's rumbling." Mr Harris glanced across at his son. "You haven't even finished your pizza. Give it here then – I think I've just got room for it."

"Er, no. I'll . . . eat it in a moment."

"I don't know what's the matter with you these days," grumbled Mr Harris. "I remember when all you needed was a takeaway and a bit of telly and you'd be happy all evening. These days, it's books and questions and homework and you don't even eat up your food."

Podge was just thinking of a reply when something made him sit up very straight in his chair. Inside his shirt, Herbert was on the move. Before Podge could do anything, a tiny rat's arm appeared between the buttons of his shirt. It pointed at the remains of the pizza and made a brisk beckoning gesture.

Quickly, Podge covered his stomach with both hands. "I think I'll just warm this up in the oven," he said, standing up carefully. Before his parents could

say anything, he hurried out to the
kitchen, carrying his plate. Wrapping
the slice of pizza in a paper towel, he
went upstairs to his room.

"Are you crazy, Herbert?" he said,
taking the rat out from his shirt.

"I only wanted some pizza," said
Herbert. "I wouldn't have minded
watching a bit of telly either."

"My dad would go mad if he saw
you."

Herbert looked away unhappily. "Funny how everyone seems to have gone off one these days. Your parents. That silly Mr Arnold. Even Ms Wiz has abandoned me. I can't understand what it is about a talking rat that people seem so uncomfortable with." He gave a long, thin sigh.

Podge stroked Herbert's head. "I'm comfortable with you," he said. "It's just that we'll have to be a bit careful now that you're staying here." He put the slice of pizza down in front of Herbert. "Eat up. It's American Hot."

"Has it got cheese?" Herbert asked in a sulky voice. "I *must* have cheese on my pizzas."

"Peter!" From downstairs, the booming voice of Mr Harris could be heard.

"Now what?" moaned Podge to himself.

"*Peter!*" Mr Harris raised his voice.

"These apples – something's been nibbling at them."

Podge groaned. "Gee thanks, Herbert," he said. "That's all I need."

Herbert was lying back on the bed, chewing slowly on his pizza, a smile on his face. "You know," he said. "I think I could get to like it here."

CHAPTER THREE

Arabella

Rats are charming, easygoing creatures.
Give them space, a nice run and lots of
food and they'll be happy. Hamsters,
gerbils and guinea pigs are all right in
their way but most sensible people
would agree that there's no pet
quite as perfect in every way as a
rat.

On the other hand, a magical talking
rat who's in a rather bad mood and
who's being hidden from parents who
can't stand any kind of animal can
sometimes be a bit of problem.

Yet, for about three weeks, Herbert's
stay with Podge Harris passed without
too much trouble.

When Podge insisted that his mother
knocked on the door before entering his

room, Mrs Harris thought it was just part of growing up.

When Mr Harris noticed that his favourite chocolate biscuits were disappearing, he assumed that Podge was the culprit.

When Lizzie, Podge's friend from Class Five at St Barnabas, took to coming round after school, Podge explained that they were doing homework together and his parents believed every word.

Neither Mr nor Mrs Harris had the faintest idea that Herbert the rat was now living in the bottom drawer of a cupboard where Podge used to keep his old toys. He had made a nest out of an old tracksuit and had carefully gnawed a hole in the back of the cupboard so that he could get in and out whenever he chose.

Podge had spent his pocket money on the fancy rat mix which Ms Wiz had mentioned and every day would bring Herbert a treat from downstairs – some cornflakes, a bit of cake or, best of all, a chocolate biscuit.

As Ms Wiz had suggested, Podge had left open the window of his bedroom, so that at night Herbert could slip out of the house, across the roof and down into the outside world. Sometimes, early in the morning, Podge would feel him tiptoeing across the bed on his return to his drawer.

Until, one morning, he didn't.

"Maybe he's run back to Ms Wiz," said Lizzie when she returned with Podge after school that day. Lizzie knew everything about animals and, of all his friends in Class Five, she had taken most interest in Herbert.

Podge shook his head. "He would have told me," he said, gazing sadly at

the empty drawer. "Perhaps he's been run over. Or got lost. What am I going to tell Ms Wiz?"

For a moment, they sat in gloomy silence. Then a sound, only slightly louder than thought, could be heard from across the room. It was a sort of humming noise and came from behind the half-closed door of a large wardrobe.

Podge and Lizzie looked at one another, then slowly approached the wardrobe. When Podge opened the door, they saw in the darkness, the pale figure of Herbert, stretched out in one of Podge's old trainers. Around his neck was a chain of forget-me-nots.

"Hi," he said dreamily.

"Where have you been, Herbert?" asked Podge. "We were so worried about you."

"If you were going to stay out the night, at least you could have told us," said Lizzie. "We were out of our minds with worry."

"You treat this place like a hotel," said Podge. "I never thought you'd be so irresponsible."

"It's not so much that you've let us down," said Lizzie. "It's that you've let yourself down. We're very disappointed."

Herbert looked coolly from Podge to Lizzie and back again. "Thank you, Mummy and Daddy," he said.

"And what are you doing in the cupboard?" asked Lizzie.

"We thought it looked cosier in here," said Herbert sleepily. "Now, if you don't mind, I'd like to catch up on my kip."

"*We*?" said Podge and Lizzie together.

It was at this moment that, from another shoe nearby, a second pair of ears emerged nervously, shyly. In the half-light, Podge and Lizzie could see another rat – one that was quite unlike Herbert. It was greyer, darker and with no white on it – the sort of rat you might see scurrying along a ditch or across a road late at night.

"Podge," muttered Lizzie beneath her breath. "I think that's a wild rat."

"Meet my new girlfriend," said Herbert proudly. "I've called her Arabella."

"Arabella?" said Podge politely. "Very posh."

"Just because she doesn't talk like you and me." Herbert's little eyes blazed angrily. "Just because she was born in a sewer, you think you can laugh at her."

"We weren't laughing," said Lizzie. "It's just that fancy rats and feral rats aren't meant to mix. I read it in a book."

"She is a bit of a wild child, it's true," said Herbert. "That's what I like about her. I'll teach her how to talk and she'll bring out my inner warrior." He smiled

at Arabella, who was staring at him with adoring eyes. She gave a little squeak of admiration.

"I think the talking might be a bit of problem," murmured Podge.

"She's different from you." Lizzie spoke gently, not wanting to hurt Herbert's feelings. "She'll probably have . . . fleas and things."

Herbert shrugged.

"What are a few blood-sucking parasites when true love comes to call?

You know what they say – love me, love my fleas." He placed a paw on his heart and gave a little cough. "In fact, I'm writing a little song for Arabella. Would you like to hear it?"

Without waiting for an answer, he began to sing in a thin, quavery voice.

"My love was born down in a sewer,
She's come up from the gutter.
She's ripe and tasty and mature,
Like cheese on bread and butter.

"Every day I love to—"

Just then there was a sharp knock on the door. Herbert and Arabella dived back into their trainers. As Mrs Harris entered, Podge shut the wardrobe door.

"You two are meant to be doing homework." Podge's mother looked around the room suspiciously. "I thought I heard some singing."

"Music," said Podge quickly. "We've been asked to write a song together."

"Go on then," said Mrs Harris. "Let's hear you."

Podge took a deep breath. "La-la-la, tum-ty-tum, blah, blah," he sang tunelessly.

"We're sort of still working on it," said Lizzie.

"Anyway, I need to clean your room," said Mrs Harris. "Something rather unpleasant seems to have happened."

Podge winced. "Unpleasant?"

"It's a bit embarrassing to have to say this in front of a nice girl like Lizzie but . . . there seems to be an invasion of mice in the house. Or maybe" – Mrs Harris shuddered – "even rats."

"Rats, yuk!" said Podge loudly, glancing in the direction of the cupboard. "How d'you know?"

"There are droppings all over the kitchen table – near the biscuits. Your dad's called in the Environmental Health Officer to deal with them. Rats in our own little house." Shaking her head, Mrs Harris turned to leave. "Who would have believed it?"

For a few seconds after the door had closed, Podge and Lizzie stood in silence.

"Did you hear that, Herbert?" Podge said quietly.

From behind the cupboard door, a faint sound of singing could be heard.

*"Every day I love to think
Of my own sweet Arabella."*

"Herbert?" said Lizzie.

"Her little eyes of—"

"Herbert!" said both Podge and Lizzie.

There was a moment's silence. "Ah

yes," Herbert mumbled in a voice that was almost embarrassed. "That was the other thing about Arabella I forgot to mention. Um . . . She's not exactly house-trained."

Love Potion Number Nine

"I'm missing her *so* much. I'm missing her from the tip of my front whiskers to the end of my tail. I'm only half a rat without her. I'm a mere shadow of my rodent self."

"Give it a break, Herbert," muttered Podge.

From his position in Podge's top pocket, Herbert the rat was talking about love as they made their way down the High Street with Lizzie.

"Just concentrate on getting us to Ms Wiz's house," said Lizzie. "Forget about Arabella for a moment."

"I wouldn't be missing her so much if you'd brought her with us," said Herbert grumpily.

"Sorry, Herb," said Podge. "Call me

old-fashioned but I'm not walking around with a street rat in my pocket."

"She's no more a street rat than you're a street child," said Herbert.

"Except I don't live in a sewer and poo on the kitchen table," muttered Podge under his breath.

"Next left!" snapped Herbert.

They walked down a quiet, leafy side street and soon were standing outside a small house, covered in ivy, which Podge recognized from the last time he had visited Ms Wiz. He rang the bell and, seconds later, the door was flung open.

"Podge! Lizzie!" Ms Wiz glanced down and her smile wavered slightly. "Herbert! What a lovely surprise. How have you been?"

Herbert cleared his throat, took a deep breath and began to sing.

"My love's a rat beyond compare.
Beside her, others pale.

I want to kiss her everywhere,
From her whiskers to her tail."

"Herbert's fallen in love," Podge explained. "And his girlfriend's living with him in my house."

"Oh, Herbert, really." Ms Wiz laughed.

"She's cute and clean and healthy too,
Entirely free from rabies.
What's more, in a week or two,
She's going to have our babies."

"What!" said Podge.

"Blimey, that was quick," said Lizzie.

"You wouldn't understand." Herbert shrugged. "It's a rat thing."

"My parents have discovered there are rats in the house," Podge told Ms Wiz. "They've called in the Environmental Health Officer."

"The world is against us but we don't care." Herbert was waving his paws around. "Love will conquer all."

Ms Wiz shook her head. "I'm not sure there's much I can do." Glancing over her shoulder, she dropped her voice. "I promised Brian I wouldn't get involved in any magic."

"Excuse me, Ms Wiz," said Podge

firmly. "You can't just deliver Herbert to me, get me into all sorts of trouble and then just wash your hands of it."

"*So* selfish," said Herbert. "Always was, always will be."

Ms Wiz thought for moment. "Wait," she said, turning back into the house. When she returned, she held a small bottle in her hand. "Put a drop of this liquid in the rat man's tea," she said. "I call it 'Love Potion Number Nine'."

"Is that because it's got nine magic ingredients?" asked Podge.

"Or is nine a special paranormal number?" asked Lizzie.

"No, it's just named after a song I used to sing when I was . . . slightly younger," said Ms Wiz.

"What does it—?"

"Sshh." Ms Wiz put a finger to her lips. "I'm sure everything will be just fine," she said, and closed the front door in their face.

"What did I tell you?" said Herbert. "It's just 'me, me, me' with that woman."

It wasn't a great plan. It wasn't even a particularly original one. But, in the end, it was the only plan that Podge and Lizzie could think of.

They would hide Herbert and Arabella in the wardrobe. They would try to get the Environmental Health Officer to take some tea. They would slip a drop of the potion Ms Wiz had given them into his cup. Then they would hope for the best.

"I'm sure it will work," said Podge as he closed the wardrobe door on the two rats.

"We just have to trust Ms Wiz," said Lizzie.

"Hah!" The voice of Herbert could be heard through the door. "That's the mistake I made. Now look where I am."

At that moment, they heard the front doorbell ring. "Don't say a word," said Podge in the general direction of the wardrobe.

By the time they had gone downstairs, a small, chubby man with a moustache had been shown into the kitchen. "Ken Duff's the name," he was saying to Mr and Mrs Harris. "I'm the council's Environmental Health Officer."

"Excellent," said Podge's father. "There are rats in the house and I want them dead." He held up a saucer on which some small droppings had been kept.

Mr Duff lowered his nose and sniffed at them. "Could be bats," he said uncertainly.

"Bats in the kitchen, eating my chocolate biscuits? Don't talk daft," said Mr Harris.

"Kettle's boiling," said Podge as

casually as he could manage. "Anyone fancy a cup of tea?"

"I'm sure Mr Duff's too busy for tea," said Mr Harris. "He's got some rats to deal with."

"Thirsty work," said Lizzie.

"Actually . . ." The Environmental Health Officer smiled at Podge and Lizzie. "A cup of tea would go down very nicely."

"Yesss!" said Podge. "I mean . . . yes, would you like sugar with it?"

"Just one spoonful," said Mr Duff.

"What d'you use?" asked Mr Harris. "Gas? Guns? Dynamite? I'll help if you want."

Mr Duff looked shocked. "Oh no, I'll just leave a little powder in the places where they feed. When they eat it, they'll go slowly to sleep."

"Tea?" Podge handed him the cup.

Mr Duff sipped at the tea and smiled.

"Mm," he said. "Does you good, doesn't it?"

"Hope so," murmured Podge.

At first, it was difficult to see how
exactly Love Potion Number Nine
worked. There was no strange humming
noise. Mr Duff didn't change in any
dramatic way after drinking the tea. He
just smiled a bit more.

"No rats here." He sounded almost relieved as he emerged from the sitting room.

"What about upstairs?" asked Mrs Harris. "Peter's room is such a mess it would be heaven for a rat."

"Actually, they're rather tidy animals," said Mr Duff, heading up the stairs.

By the time he had reached Podge's room, he had begun to act rather

strangely. He looked at the clothes on the floor, at the pile of papers on the desk, at the unmade bed, and smiled broadly. "What a *lovely* room," he said.

"Eh?" said Podge.

As if by instinct, he went straight to the wardrobe and looked down at the shoes. There, trying to make themselves look small, were Herbert and Arabella.

Podge was just about to explain that they were his secret pets when Mr Duff looked more closely at the rats.

"*Sweet*," he murmured. "And I do believe this little darling's pregnant."

"Little darling?" Lizzie glanced at Podge. "I thought you were meant to be . . . getting rid of them."

"Get rid of them? What a terrible thought. It's a privilege for you to have those adorable little creatures in the house."

Lizzie glanced at Podge. "I think the

potion might be working," she murmured.

"Any luck?" Mrs Harris put her head around the door as Mr Duff stood up and closed the wardrobe door behind him.

For a moment, he stared at Mrs Harris. Then a bashful smile appeared on his face. "Has anyone told you that you're the most beautiful woman in the world?"

A few moments later, he was thrown out on to the street.

CHAPTER FIVE

Stiff City, Ratwise

It was 3.22 the following afternoon when a white van with darkened windows, marked *Killing Fields Pest Control*, turned into Rylett Road and stopped outside the Harrises' house. Three men in white overalls, baseball caps and heavy boots stepped out and trudged up the garden path.

"Thank goodness you're here," said Mr Harris, who was standing at the front door. "We called out an exterminator from the council but they sent round a nutter. He fell in love with my wife."

"I thought he was rather nice," said Mrs Harris from the hall. "He had gentle eyes."

"Never mind gentle eyes," said the

smallest of the three men. "My name's Dave Fields. In the trade, they call me 'Killing' Fields."

Podge appeared at the front door, a mug in his hands. "The kettle's just boiled, Mr . . . er, Killing," he said. "D'you fancy a cup of tea?"

"Tea?" Dave Fields laughed nastily. "We're exterminators. We don't drink tea."

"*He* did, my Ken." Mrs Harris was staring into the distance. "He sipped in a very . . . sensitive way."

Ignoring her, Dave Fields scanned the front garden with narrowed eyes. "We're going in hard and we're going in fast," he said. "Gas, poison. Outside the house and in. In ten minutes' time, this place will be Stiff City, ratwise. He pointed to a manhole nearby. "We'll start there."

Beside Podge, Lizzie gave a little moan. Herbert and Arabella had disappeared, there was no sign of Ms Wiz and there seemed little hope of the men falling for the old love potion trick. "Are you sure you wouldn't like some tea?" she said. "It's really—"

She paused. At that moment, a strange humming noise could be heard. It was getting louder all the time.

Together the three men looked down the street.

A shape, a sort of black and yellow cloud, was approaching. Outside the house, it paused and made its way up the garden path, the hum becoming an angry buzz.

"Blimey, wasps," said one of the men. "Where did they come from?"

Podge nudged Lizzie. "Nice one, Ms Wiz," he whispered.

The wasps grew closer, moving to one side of the path. They surrounded the three men, forcing them back towards the van.

"Where are you off to?" shouted Mr
Harris. "I thought you were meant to
be a hit squad."

Casually, Dave Fields reached
through the window of the van. When
he faced the wasps, he was carrying a
large gas canister.

"Wasp gas." He smiled unpleasantly,
pointed it at the swarm of wasps and
pressed a button. A grey cloud
enveloped the wasps. When it cleared,
the buzzing had died down. Where the
wasps had been stood a familiar figure,
coughing and wiping tears from her eyes.

"Great magic, Ms Wiz," muttered
Podge.

"Unfair," wheezed Ms Wiz. "That was
gas – it could have been really nasty."

"It's that fruit-seller again," said Mr
Harris. "Where did she come from?"

"Clear off, lady." Dave Fields put the
gas canister back in the van. "This is
men's work."

"Men's work, eh?" From behind Ms Wiz, a humming sound could just be heard. It grew louder and louder ... then suddenly began to falter, like an engine misfiring, before fading into silence.

Ms Wiz shook her head helplessly. "I seem to be a bit out of practice these days," she muttered. "I had a spell prepared but it doesn't seem to be working."

"Right," said Dave. "We're going in."

"Halt!"

A thin, well-educated voice, coming from just beyond the manhole, cut the air. The three men hesitated.

"Halt!"

And there, on the garden wall, with Arabella beside him, was Herbert. He was standing on his hind legs, one paw on his heart, the other before him, like a rat general addressing his troops before a great battle.

"Am I dreaming, Dave?" said one of the men. "Or is that a talking rat on the wall?"

"Why do you wish to destroy my people – my wife's family?" Herbert raised his voice. "Have they harmed you in any way? No! Rats and men have lived together for thousands of years. You need us. We help clear up the mess humans leave behind."

"Horrid, dirty things," said Mr Harris.

"Dirty?" Herbert put his tiny arm around Arabella. "Does this divine little thing look dirty to you? Will the babies that she is carrying, who one day will call me 'Daddy' – will they be horrid?"

"I've heard enough of this." Dave Fields stepped forward and extended a big gloved hand towards the wall.

Suddenly, with a loud, angry chattering sound, Arabella moved to stand in front of Herbert. Rearing up on her hind legs, eyes blazing, fangs bared, she was a truly terrifying sight.

"So much for the divine little thing," said Lizzie.

Dave Field had turned pale. "Give us a hand, lads," he called over his shoulder.

As the other two men moved forward, Herbert seemed to take a deep breath. He extended both paws – and began to sing.

"Rats in love, rats in love,
We're different yet the same.
Ours is the secret, special love
That dare not squeak its name."

"Aah," said Mrs Harris. "Isn't that sweet?"

"Sweet? It's rubbish," said Mr Harris. But there was a crack in his voice which Podge had never heard before.

"Every day I love to think
Of my lovely Arabella.
Her eyes are of the brightest pink,
Her teeth are shining yellow."

One of the men sniffed. Another seemed to be wiping something from the corner of his eye.

"I'll marry her when the sun shines,
I'll marry her in the rain,
And then, when no one's looking,
I'll marry her again."

"I'm off home," said one of the men.
"Me too," said the other.
Dave shrugged. "They're almost

human," he said, turning to Mr Harris.
"Sorry, mate. Can't do it."

"Cuthbert." Mrs Harris laid a hand
on her husband's arm. "They remind
me of us when we were courting."

"What's going on?" Mr Harris
shouted angrily as the men returned to
their van. "I thought you were meant
to be a hit squad."

But, with a slamming of doors and a
roar of the engine, the Killing Fields van
drew away and was gone.

"Well done, Ms Wiz," smiled Podge.

"Wiz?" Mr Harris narrowed his eyes.
"I knew I recognized you from
somewhere. You're that Wiz woman
who's always causing spells and magic
and . . . trouble."

Absent-mindedly, he reached for the
mug in Podge's hand.

"Dad . . ." Podge shouted.

But it was too late. Mr Harris drained
the lot in three angry gulps.

"Actually, it wasn't me or my magic." Ms Wiz smiled politely. "It was Herbert and Arabella and" – she shrugged helplessly – "true love."

"I told you love conquers all," said Herbert. "Sometimes being right all the time can be positively boring."

"There's one thing it hasn't conquered," said Podge. "And that's the problem of where Herbert and Arabella and all their little babies are going to live."

Ms Wiz gathered up the two rats in her hands. "If they live outside our house and visit us now and then, I'm sure I can convince Brian to change his mind. He's an old romantic at heart."

Herbert held open the fold of Ms Wiz's coat for his wife. "After you, my dear," he said. She scuttled out of sight. Herbert gave a little wave in the direction of Podge and Lizzie.

"Toodle-oo, chaps," he said. "Thanks for

having us." Then he disappeared.

"See you both soon." Ms Wiz smiled, turning to leave.

"Not so fast, young lady." Mr Harris laid a hand on her shoulder. "I've got something to say to you."

"Dad, she hasn't done you any harm," said Podge.

"Oh, but she has." Mr Harris seemed to be blushing as he gazed at Ms Wiz. "You see . . . I think I've fallen in love with her."

"Oh." Ms Wiz backed away nervously. "That's nice."

"I know it's a bit sudden but it's the real thing." Mr Harris gave a sort of giggle. "I'm in love."

"Isn't that great, Cuthbert?" said Mrs Harris. "I'm in love, too. All I can think about is that sweet Ken Duff."

"I think I'd better be going," said Ms Wiz.

"Hang on," said Podge. "Thanks to

your precious Love Potion Number Nine, we don't have any rats here but we've got a love riot on our hands."

"It'll fade after about a week," said Ms Wiz.

"A *week*?" said Lizzie.

As Ms Wiz closed the garden gate behind her, the voice of Herbert, muffled but happy, could be heard.

"My love was born down in a sewer,
She's come up from the gutter.
She's ripe and tasty and mature
Like cheese on bread and butter."

"Don't go, darling Ms Wiz," Mr Harris called out.

"Ken," murmured Mrs Harris. "I must see my Ken."

"Help," said Podge.

Ms Wiz and the
Sister of Doom

For Tom Charleston

CHAPTER ONE
The One and Only

It was a dark and stormy morning. Low, wispy clouds raced across the sky as if they were late for a meeting. The wind whispered secrets through the winter trees which stood like skeletons in the park. Jack Beddows ignored it all as he made his sleepy way towards St Barnabas School.

A black cat scurried across his path and disappeared into some bushes. "Yo, cat," Jack muttered.

A magpie on a railing scolded what sounded like a warning as he walked by. "Cool it, birdie," said Jack, as he walked under a high ladder that was leaning against a building.

He turned the corner into St

Barnabas Road and almost bumped into his friend Caroline Smith, who was standing on the pavement, writing something in a notebook. "Bit late to start your homework now, Cazza," he said.

"It's not homework," said Caroline impatiently. "I'm making notes in my nature diary."

"Nature? In the middle of this town?" Jack laughed. "Maybe you should come round to my place. Our cat has some really interesting fleas."

Caroline nodded in the direction of the school and now Jack saw what she had been looking at. On the roof, standing as still as soldiers on parade, was a row of large, black birds.

"Wow," he said. "Vultures. They must have got a whiff of the school kitchen."

"Carrion crows, actually," said

Caroline, licking her pencil. "That's . . . thirteen carrion crows on the school roof, seen on . . ." she checked the date, "Friday the thirteenth of December."

"Hey, coincidence," said Jack.

Shortly after the bell of St Barnabas School sounded for morning assembly, a long, black car with the number plate BABS 13 drew up outside the school gates. A tall, blonde woman stepped out of the driver's seat and walked round to open the other door. From there, a pale, skinny man in a black suit emerged. The woman seemed to straighten the back of his coat before walking slowly with him through the gates.

As the two of them crossed the playground, the crows on the roof set

up a loud chorus of cawing and flapped their wings, making a sound like wet sheets blowing in the wind. The woman raised both hands and the white of her nail varnish seemed to glow in the morning gloom. Within seconds the birds were still.

The two dark figures entered the school.

The end of the winter term had always been a difficult time of the year for Mr Gilbert. Ever since he had become headteacher at St Barnabas, the month of December had brought problems. Sometimes parents were angry with him because their child was only playing a donkey in the nativity play. Or maybe Mrs Gilbert was annoyed with him for buying a Christmas tree that was too small or too big, or one whose needles all fell off as soon as he got it home. Then there was always a row over which teacher should look after Class Two's gerbils over the holidays.

Frankly, the last thing he needed right now was important visitors arriving at the school without any warning.

"We are part of a government task force looking into education," the blonde woman told him when they were shown into his study.

"Ah." Mr Gilbert smiled politely. "Which one?"

"Witch?" The woman narrowed her eyes. "Who mentioned a witch? We're perfectly ordinary education inspectors."

She nudged the man who had accompanied her.

"Ordinary education inspectors," he said in a deep, distant voice.

"Now, all we need to do is chat to some of the children. I'll do that while my colleague Derek will stay with you."

"Stay with you," said the man.

"We're all terribly busy at this time of the year," said Mr Gilbert. "There are plays to put on, and end-of-term reports. Then there's the whole gerbil problem."

The woman smiled dangerously. "I wish I had time to tell you just how little I care about your gerbil problems." She stood up. "Oh, and there was one other thing." Without warning, the room seemed to fill with a sharp crackling noise. Mr Gilbert's head slumped forward. His eyes closed. Within seconds, he was fast asleep.

"One other thing," intoned Derek, his eyes blank and unseeing.

Mr Bailey, Class Five's teacher, was tired. The children always grew difficult and rowdy as the end of term approached and this term was no exception.

So he was quite pleased when a tall, blonde woman knocked on the door and told him that she was part of a government task force and that Mr Gilbert, the headteacher, had suggested she meet Class Five. At least it meant he didn't have to teach for a few minutes.

He drew up a chair beside his desk. "Take a pew, Miss . . ."

"You can call me madam."

But Mr Bailey was looking more closely at the visitor. "Madam?" He smiled. "Don't you mean Ms? You've changed the colour of your hair and that nail varnish of yours used to be black but I do believe you're our old friend—"

Suddenly a sharp, crackling noise could be heard. Mr Bailey widened his eyes briefly, then slumped back in his chair, snoring loudly.

"Goodness me," said the woman.

"Your teacher seems to have nodded off."

For a moment there was silence in the classroom.

"Of course, he was right." The woman smiled brightly. "I'm back. Isn't it great?"

"Ms Wiz?" There was uncertainty in Caroline's voice.

"Yup." The woman nodded. "The one and only."

"You look sort of . . . different," said Jack.

"*What*?" The woman's eyes flashed angrily. "Are you saying I'm not as pretty as my . . ." she hesitated, "as I once was?"

"Maybe it's the blond hair," said Jack.

The woman seemed to have regained control of herself. "It's what they call a make-over," she said.

"But why are you here?" asked Podge Harris. "I thought you were Mrs Arnold, looking after baby William and not doing any magic these days."

The woman smiled coldly. "Witches don't need reasons," she said.

Podge and Jack looked at one another in surprise.

"But you always said that 'witch' was an old-fashioned word and gave people the wrong idea," said Podge. "That was why you called yourself a paranormal op—"

The loud, angry, crackling noise filled the room once more. Podge swayed for a moment, as if caught by a sudden gust of wind. Then he began to shrink, seeming to grow a bright shade of orange as he did so. Soon, all there was to be seen on his seat was a large pumpkin.

"Thanks, fat boy. Pumpkin pie's my
favourite." The woman walked to the
back of the class, picked up the
pumpkin and put it in her shoulder
bag.

"Nice trick, Ms Wiz," said Jack with
a hint of panic in his voice. "Except
you always promised that magic
would be used for good things."

"That's the thing about coming
from the other side." The woman

walked briskly to the door. "We change. Sometimes we're paranormal operatives, but then sometimes we go back to being a good old witchety witch. In the past you've seen my generous side. Now" – she opened the door – "it's no more Ms Nice Guy." She slammed the door behind her.

Caroline hurried to Mr Bailey and shook him awake.

"Wha-what happened?" he muttered. "I was having a nightmare about teaching Class Five." He looked around him. "Oh no. It was true."

"Ms Wiz has gone all weird," said Caroline.

"Tell me something I don't know," said Mr Bailey.

"She's turned Podge into a great big, fat pumpkin," said Katrina.

"Oh, really? How could you tell?" Mr Bailey laughed at his own joke.

"And kidnapped him," added Jack.

Suddenly Mr Bailey looked more concerned. "Oh dear," he said.

"Look!" shouted Lizzie, pointing out of the window. Walking quickly across the playground were the two dark figures. Class Five watched as the woman stopped and seemed to fiddle with something at the back of the man's neck. As if he were a balloon, he shrivelled up until he was a little pile of clothes on the ground. The woman picked him up, put him in her bag, walked to her car and drove off. Behind the car flew thirteen carrion crows.

"Oh dear, oh dear," said Mr Bailey.

CHAPTER TWO
Just a Zombie Slave

By the end of that day, St Barnabas School was in an uproar. Mr Bailey had hurried to the headteacher's office to explain what had happened while he had unfortunately fallen asleep during class, only to find that Mr Gilbert was asleep as well. The caretaker, Mr Brown, had been asked to look in all the cupboards and bins in the school grounds just in case a large pumpkin had been left there. The police had been called in. Soon the school was alive with rumours.

Ms Wiz was back!

Ms Wiz had gone bonkers!

Ms Wiz had turned Podge into a pumpkin and kidnapped him!

At lunchtime, Mr Gilbert nervously picked up the telephone and rang the town hall, where Podge's father, Mr Harris, worked.

"Ah, hello, Mr Harris," he said, trying to sound calm. "I'm afraid we have a bit of a problem with young Peter. No, no, he hasn't done anything wrong. It's just that there has been, well, some rather unfortunate magic and he seems to have disappeared with our old friend Ms Wiz . . . Yes, sorry. Please don't swear, Mr Harris. How? Er, well, there's one other thing which I have to tell you . . ."

"Changed into a *pumpkin*?"

It was after school and Jack and Caroline were sitting in a small kitchen. Across the table from them, looking like she always did, only slightly more worried, was Ms Wiz.

"Yes," said Jack. "Then she put him into this big bag and carried him off."

"We hoped it had been you playing a trick on us," said Caroline.

"Lizzie said that she read somewhere that Friday the thirteenth is a sort of paranormal version of April Fool's Day," said Jack.

"Friday the thirteenth." Ms Wiz had gone deathly pale. "That's my sister's birthday."

Jack and Caroline looked at one another in amazement.

"Your sister?" said Jack. "We never knew you had a family."

"Mm?" Ms Wiz was still frowning. "Of course I've got a family. I've got eighteen lovely sisters."

"*Eighteen*?" said Jack.

"How did your parents manage

that?" asked Caroline.

"Well, when mummies and daddies want to have a baby, they get together and—"

"Thank you, Ms Wiz," said Jack quickly. "We know where babies come from."

"Well, I've got eighteen lovely sisters. We look exactly the same, and we all go wherever we're needed. There's Señorita Wiziana in Ecuador,

Miss Wazza in Australia, Ms
用 邪 法 个 女 人
in China. Magic knows no boundaries."

"The woman who came to school didn't seem exactly lovely," muttered Caroline.

"Eighteen lovely sisters." Ms Wiz spoke distantly, as if she was remembering things she would rather

have forgotten. "And one who is not quite so lovely. She was the thirteenth sister and, by a tragic accident, she was born on December the thirteenth under a full moon – and that can only mean one thing. She's nothing but trouble. Her idea of a good time is to sink a few ships, whip up a hurricane or invent a really nasty disease. She was always a difficult little girl but she has grown up to be the embodiment of evil. They call her . . . Barbara."

"Scary name," Jack murmured.

Ms Wiz sighed. "How *could* I have forgotten to send her a birthday card?"

"But why did she pick on you?" asked Caroline. "She could have visited Ms Wiziana or Miss Wazza."

"She was always jealous of me. Jealous of my friends. Jealous of my spells. Jealous of my exceptionally good looks."

Jack and Caroline looked at one another.

"I thought she was rather nice-looking," said Jack.

"Huh, you haven't seen her ankles. As for that ridiculous blond hair."

"It wasn't her fault she was the thirteenth sister and born on Friday the thirteenth," said Caroline, thinking of her own little sister. "With all that going on, she was always going to be a bit . . . dodgy."

"*Dodgy*?" Ms Wiz gave an angry little laugh. "She always had to be the special one, with her wicked spells and her silly blood-curdling curses. And we all had to be *really* frightened of her just because she had the deadly mark of everlasting evil upon her. I know one should put it down to attention-seeking, but there is a limit."

"And I suppose that creepy bloke with her is your brother-in-law," said Jack.

Ms Wiz shook her head impatiently "He's no one."

"He looked like someone to me," muttered Jack. "Someone I'd very much prefer not to see again."

"No, I meant he really is no one – he doesn't exist," said Ms Wiz casually. "He's just one of my sister's zombie slaves."

"Oh, fine, just a zombie slave." Jack gulped. "That's all right then."

Ms Wiz sighed. "The problem is that, if we don't move fast, Podge could become a zombie slave himself."

"Oh, Podge!" moaned Jack.

"We?" said Caroline. "Did you just say 'we'?"

*

148

At first, when Caroline's mother Mrs Smith returned from dropping off her younger daughter at a party to find the house empty, she was not too alarmed. Caroline was playing an angel in the school play and she sometimes had to stay late for rehearsals.

In fact, it was only when the telephone rang five minutes later that she really began to worry.

"I don't want you to panic." Caroline's voice sounded breathless. "But there's been a bit of an emergency."

"An emergency? Are you all right?"

"I'm fine – but Podge isn't. He's . . . sort of disappeared."

"*Sort* of disappeared? What's going on, Caroline?"

"It's a bit of a long story, Mum. All you need to know is that I'm in safe hands. Jack and I are with Ms Wiz."

"Oh no, not her again. The last time I saw that woman she shrank you and took you inside the television set. Talk about irresponsible. Anyway, I thought that these days she was Mrs Dolores Arnold – all married and settled down."

"She is, but even her husband Mr Arnold has agreed that this is such an emergency that it needs magic. So she's coming out of retirement."

"But what are you doing?"
Somehow the mention of Ms Wiz's
name seemed to make Mrs Smith even
more alarmed. "Where are you
going?"

"It's complicated, Mum. But we'll
be back tomorrow. Wish us luck."

"But you haven't even got your
toothbrush. Or a clean pair of—"

"Thanks, Mum," said Caroline.

And she was gone.

"As a matter of interest, where *are* we
going?" Caroline asked Ms Wiz. They
had kissed baby William goodbye, told
Mr Arnold they would be back soon
and closed the front door behind them.

"It has different names," said Ms
Wiz as she walked down her path.
"Some people call it the 'Other Side' or
the 'Dark Beyond'."

"I really don't like the sound of this," said Jack, hanging back.

"Personally I prefer to call it the 'Underworld'."

"Underworld?" said Caroline. "I get claustrophobia in a basement."

Ms Wiz was waiting by the side of the road. She held out each of her hands. "Hold on, both of you," she said. "This is a very busy road."

"I think we're old enough to cross a road," said Jack.

There was a distant humming noise. "Hold my hand, quick!" shouted Ms Wiz.

As each of them touched Ms Wiz's hands, Jack and Caroline felt a jolt passing through their bodies, like a giant heartbeat. They heard a whistling in their ears. And suddenly everything went dark.

CHAPTER THREE
The Purple Room

When Jack and Caroline opened their
eyes, they were dazzled by whiteness.
It was as if they were in a vast winter
wonderland, or a white desert where
the white sand stretched to a white
horizon where it met a white sky.
There was no colour or shade or
darkness or shape wherever they
looked. Even the air they breathed
seemed to smell white.

"Er, Ms Wiz," said Jack, slowly
taking his hands from his eyes.
"Would you mind telling me where
we are?"

"We are beyond space and time,
between the real world and the
underworld." Ms Wiz's voice sounded

strange and muffled. "Now we'd better hurry up or we'll be late."

Caroline frowned. "How can we be late if we're beyond time and space?"

"Because it's a long way," said Ms Wiz.

"No, I'm sorry," said Caroline firmly. "But if there's no time and space here, then things like 'a long way' and 'being late' are meaningless."

Ms Wiz glanced at Jack. "Is she always like this?" she asked.

"She's been reading a lot of books recently," Jack explained. "Sometimes when she starts talking in class, time really does stand still. I nodded off once and when I woke up she was still in the same sentence."

Ms Wiz was looking around her. She put her fingers to her lips and gave a long, low whistle. The sound died in the still air about them. Then silence returned.

Suddenly Caroline screamed. "Something touched my ankle!" She grabbed Jack's arm. "It was all soft and spooky."

There was a soft crackling sound, like the noise made by a sparkler, just in front of where they stood. Slowly, dark patches formed against the whiteness. They began to take shape. After a few seconds, a very old black and white cat appeared. It scratched itself lazily behind the ear.

"Ah, Cerberus, there you are." Ms Wiz smiled as she stroked the cat.

"Cerberus?" Caroline frowned. "Wasn't that the name of the dog in the Greek legends who had three heads and guarded the gates of hell?"

Ms Wiz laughed. "You and your books, Caroline. Cerberus is a cat.

And, as you can see, he only has one head."

"What about the guarding the gates of hell bit?" asked Jack.

"Well, we'd better be going," said Ms Wiz quickly.

Cerberus had sat down and was gazing into space. The white air in front of him seemed to part, revealing a small purple room, containing three white armchairs.

"Cats have special powers," Ms Wiz said quietly. "No one can enter the underworld without Cerberus's help." She stepped into the room and turned to the cat.

"We'll be wanting Level Thirteen," she said.

Cerberus hissed and raised his hackles.

"It's all right. We won't be staying long." Ms Wiz turned to Jack and

Caroline. "My sister isn't very popular down here," she explained.

As soon as all four of them were in the room, the doors closed behind them. Seconds later they felt themselves moving downwards, faster and faster, like a pebble falling from the sky.

"Going down," Ms Wiz sang out.

Caroline slumped into one of the chairs. "I wonder what Mum's doing," she sighed.

Mrs Smith had rung the police. Then she had rung Jack's mother who said that she was sure that the children would be safe with Ms Wiz. Then she had rung Podge's father who had shouted so loudly that she almost dropped the telephone. But it was when she met the policeman in charge of the case that she really began to worry.

"Detective Constable Sidney Burton at your service." A trim, grey-haired man in a dark suit stood at her door that evening. He might have been a businessman, if it were not for the large gold earring that dangled from his right ear. "I am the local psychic detective who'll be looking for the three missing kiddies. Now if I could just ask you—"

"Er, *psychic* detective?" said Mrs Smith.

"Oh yes, we do a lot of paranormal work in the modern police force. You'd be surprised how much crime is being done by dark forces. That's when I get called in. They call me 'Psychic Sid'. The man put both hands to his forehead and half-closed his eyes. "I'm getting a vibration that your

daughter is called . . . Caroline?"

Mrs Smith sighed heavily. "That's because I left her name at the station," she said.

"I thought so. My vibrations never let me down." The detective took out a notebook. "I'll be needing Caroline's relevant details. Star sign. Position on the astral plane. Lucky number."

"Are you sure this is normal police procedure?"

"What is normal? What is procedure? It's all a mystery, isn't it, madam? That's why we intend to meet this evening in the classroom at St Barnabas – on the exact spot where the boy Harris was turned into a pumpkin. We'll all hold hands and try to reach the other side to find out where they are."

"The other side of what?"

"The other side of reality, madam."

Mrs Smith shook her head. "All right, I'll be there," she said.

The purple room was beginning to slow down. Shimmering in the air at the centre of the room, as if lit by laser beam, was a sequence of rapidly changing numbers. *20 . . . 19 . . . 18 . . .*

"I wish you could meet some of my sisters," Ms Wiz said absently. "You'd love Señorita Wiziana. As for my Chinese sister, Ms

用 邪 法 个 女 人

– she's a laugh a minute. But we just don't have time."

At that moment, the number 13 hovered in front of them. While the other numbers had all been different bright colours, this was the darkest black. As the room slowed down, a

strange, unearthly sound reached
them through its walls – hammering,
clanging, echoing, with an occasional
almost human moan. The room came
to rest with a bump.

"Welcome to the underworld," said
Ms Wiz.

Slowly, the doors drew back . . .

CHAPTER FOUR
Pumpkin Pie

They were in a vast dark cavern. An odd smell, smoky yet damp, like mouldering leaves on a bonfire, hung in the air. Around the walls, by the light of flickering candles, hundreds of men and women were working at long metal benches. Not one of them looked up as Ms Wiz stepped out of the purple room.

"Zombie slaves at work," Ms Wiz said casually. "My sister does like to put on a nice show for visitors."

"We'll wait here with old Cerberus," Jack called out. "Say hi to your sister for us."

But Caroline was following Ms Wiz. "Zombie slaves are probably like tigers.

The important thing is not to let them know that you're fright— Aaaagggh!" Her scream echoed off the walls of the cavern. "Something ran over my foot."

"It's only a zombie rat," said Ms Wiz casually. "It doesn't really exist. Barbara's just showing off."

Jack was standing near a group of slave zombies. "They're making little mirrors," he said. "Maybe we could take one back as a souvenir."

"Except these mirrors break as soon as you look at them," said Ms Wiz grimly. "And over there" – she pointed to the other side of the cave – "they'll be making invisible ladders that you could walk under without noticing. Or putting tiny cracks in paving stones which people tread on without realizing."

"It's a sort of bad luck factory," said Caroline.

"Yup. This is where they breed all the black cats in the world."

"Oh come on, Ms Wiz." Jack laughed. "We've got a black cat. You're not telling me that Dodger came from the underworld."

"You look into his eyes when you get back," said Ms Wiz. "You'll see what I mean."

She was standing in front of a small wooden door which had been built into one of the walls of the cavern. On it, painted in red, was the number 13. She had hardly knocked on the door once when it swung open. The tall, blonde woman Jack and Caroline had last seen at St Barnabas stood before them.

"Why, Dolores," she said, kissing Ms Wiz on both cheeks. "What a delightful surprise."

"Hi, Barbara. And don't pretend you haven't been watching us," said

Ms Wiz coolly. "I believe you have already met my friends Jack and Caroline."

Barbara stepped forward and shook hands, first with Caroline, then with Jack. "Enchanted," she said, adding beneath her breath, "Or at least you soon will be." She turned, calling over her shoulder, "Do come in. We were just having tea. Pumpkin pie."

"P-pumpkin?" Jack stammered. "It's not Podge, is it? All his life he loved pies. Now he's become one."

Barbara laughed. "Not *that* pumpkin, Jack. What d'you think I am – some kind of monster?" She opened the door and ushered them into what seemed to be a small, neat, normal sitting room.

A single figure sat alone on a dark red sofa by a blazing fire. He had a cup of tea in his hand and was smiling vacantly. It was Podge.

"Yo, Podgey boy," Jack laughed.

Podge, smiling and staring ahead of him, took a sip of his tea but said nothing.

"He's tired after his journey," said Barbara. "Come on, Podge, don't you want to say hi?"

"Hi," said Podge, his voice distant and lifeless.

"Something's wrong, Ms Wiz," Caroline whispered over her shoulder.

There was no reply.

"Ms—?"

Her words were lost as a sharp crackling noise filled the room.

"Barbara, no!" Ms Wiz held up a hand, but even as she did so, she began to shrink and flatten and become oddly bristly. Soon, in the place where she had been standing, there lay, steaming slightly, a doormat.

"Why, Dolores, what a lovely surprise. This was just what I wanted for my birthday. I'll always treasure it." Giggling like a little girl, Barbara walked to the doormat and deliberately wiped her feet on it.

"But you can't do that," said Jack. "Ms Wiz is the one who does spells. She doesn't get changed into things."

"Except when she's on Level 13. In this part of the underworld, I have power over all living things. It's so typical of my sister to forget that. She always was the absent-minded one. Now she's not so much Ms Wiz as – " Barbara cackled – "Ms Was."

"You mean, she can't free herself?" Caroline asked.

"Nope." Barbara shrugged her shoulders skittishly. "I'm afraid we are a bit of a mad family," she said. "We do love our little jokes." She sat down on

the other side from Podge and picked
up the teapot. "Now don't stand on
ceremony. Take a seat and we'll have
some nice tea. After all, we've got so
much to discuss, haven't we?"

Nervously, Jack and Caroline
lowered themselves onto the sofa.

They were alone.

They were in the underworld.

And Ms Wiz had been turned into a
doormat.

"Now." Barbara poured the tea.
"One lump or two?"

CHAPTER FIVE
A Brand New Ms Wiz

It was late evening when the worried parents of Podge, Jack and Caroline gathered in Class Five's classroom at St Barnabas with Mr Gilbert and Mr Bailey. The paranormal investigator, Detective Constable Sidney Burton, better known as Psychic Sid, stood in front of the blackboard, a crystal ball in his hand.

"Ladies and gentlemen, we shall shortly be making contact with the other side," he announced. "I shall ask you to gather around the lad Harris's desk and place your hands on the special magic crystal. Our energies will then help me reach the astral plane where I shall endeavour to pursue my investigations."

"Astral plane. Magic crystals. Detectives wearing earrings. I've seen it all now," muttered Mr Harris.

"What happens if you actually meet the dark forces on the astral plane?" asked Mr Bailey.

"Dark forces?" Psychic Sid looked worried. "Er, well, should I actually meet one of the undead, I shall ask him to accompany me down to the station so that he can be eliminated from police enquiries. Right, gather round, everyone."

In the depths of the underworld, Jack and Caroline were experiencing the worst tea party of their lives.

"But, children, you are not drinking your tea," said Barbara in a voice which was as twinkly and innocent as that of a favourite aunt.

Caroline glanced at Podge who was still staring into space. "To tell the truth, when one of your friends has become a slave zombie and the other has been turned into a doormat, tea suddenly doesn't seem that important," she said.

Barbara chuckled. "Don't worry about my little tricks," she said. "Nothing is for ever – not even in the underworld. Of course you can take your plump little friend back. All you have to do is agree to be my friends."

"What, like penfriends?" said Jack.

"Not exactly." Her eyes grew distant. "You see, I've never really had friends, like my sisters did. Even when they were little girls they used to have parties and magic spell competitions. I tried to . . ." Barbara gave a little giggle, "enter into the spirit of things.

I'd release vampire bats in their bedrooms, or slip deadly nightshade into a birthday cake, or turn their favourite cats into werewolves – you know, the usual innocent, childish pranks. But they never let me join in. I was always a bit different."

"I can see that," muttered Caroline.

"So I decided that you and all the children of St Barnabas would be my friends. I'd invite you to tea and then you could ask me to come back to school now and then. Dolores has had such fun with you in the past. Now it's my turn. I'll be your brand new Ms Wiz, only better. I'll be there whenever magic is needed – and sometimes even when it isn't."

Before Jack or Caroline could say anything, Barbara stood up and did a little dance around the room. "I'm going to be a paranormal operative like the others," she chuckled. "And to prove it . . ." She stopped in front of Podge, laid a hand on his head and began chanting, *"Malleus mallificarum transformatum Podgus fatboy normalus."*

There was a sharp crackling sound. Podge's whole body was lifted from the chair for a few seconds. When it came back to rest, Podge shook his head and looked around him, as if waking from a long sleep. "Hey, I'm starving."

Jack laughed out loud. "Yo, Podge is back," he said.

"Where am I?" Podge was looking around him. "What hap—"

"Well, that's settled," interrupted Barbara. "We're all friends. I'll see you again soon and you can bring all the other nice little children from your class to the underworld now and then. The next time you see Ms Wiz, it will

be – " she gave a little shudder of
excitement – "*moi.*"

"What about the real Ms Wiz?"
asked Jack. "She's got a husband and a
baby and a home."

"Do they need a doormat?" Barbara
asked cheerfully. "I'm sure something
could be arranged."

"Couldn't you bring her back so
that we can say goodbye to her?"
asked Jack.

Barbara waved her right arm airily.

"Oh, you can say goodbye to her as she is. Just give her a little wipe as you leave." She stood up and showed them into the hall with impatient little brushing movements.

"There was one thing," said Jack casually. "I was wondering if I could have your autograph. I've got a few celebrities but I haven't got a real, live queen of the underworld in my book yet."

Barbara blushed. "Oh, I wouldn't say queen. More like a . . . sort of princess, really. I'll go and get a pen."

As she turned back into the sitting room, Jack grabbed the doormat and, before Podge could protest, he pushed it under his jersey. "Go!"

"Eh? I'm not nicking doormats."

But Caroline had taken Podge by the arm and had pushed him briskly out of the door.

"Here we are." Barbara returned, carrying a bit of paper. "I've put 'To Jack, Happy Spells, from your new Ms Wiz'."

"Cheers," said Jack, backing out of the door. "I'll always treasure it."

"Bye!" Barbara waved gaily and closed the door.

Podge was looking at the cavern of the underworld. "What *is* this place?" he muttered.

"Tell you later," hissed Jack.

"There's Cerberus!" Caroline laughed with relief as the black and white cat lazily stood up, giving a soft miaow of welcome.

"OK, Cerb," shouted Jack. "We're outta here – and fast!"

The cat stood up, stretched and yawned. There was a faint crackling sound and two invisible doors drew back to reveal a purple room. They were about to jump in when they heard a deafening roar of rage behind them.

"My mat! Where is my mat?"

A terrifying figure stood in the middle of the cavern – two metres tall, hands reaching out like great, scaly claws, eyes shining blood-red in the gloom. It was Barbara.

"I want my sister! I will have my sister!" All around her, the zombie slaves stopped working and turned their vacant eyes on the three children. The walls and floor of the cave seemed suddenly to come alive, writhing with snakes and huge, scurrying spiders. *"Bring back my sister!"*

Caroline took a deep breath. "I thought you were going to be a nice, friendly paranormal operative from now on," she called out.

"Nice? Me? That'll be the day!" With huge, slow steps, Barbara advanced

towards them, hundreds of her zombie slaves following her.

"But you said—"

"Not now, Caroline!" Jack pushed her and Podge into the purple room. "Doors, Cerberus!" he screamed.

As Barbara approached, the doors drew slowly to a close. At the last minute Cerberus the cat jumped out to leave Jack, Caroline and Podge alone as the room began to rise.

"Would someone mind telling me why I've got a doormat stuffed up my jumper?" asked Podge.

But, before there was time for an answer, the purple room began hurtling upwards, dissolving to whiteness as it went.

The meeting organized by Detective Constable Sidney Burton was not going too well. He had asked whether anybody was out there but there had been no reply. He had told the spirit world to move the crystal ball but it had remained still.

"I shall ask you one more time," he intoned. "Is there anyone out there who knows the whereabouts of three lost children, one of whom may be disguised as a pumpkin?"

A loud crackling sound could be heard at the back of the classroom. Parents, teachers and Psychic Sid stared in amazement as a white cloud ascended through the floorboards. It cleared slowly to reveal Jack, Caroline and Podge.

"B-blimey." Psychic Sid was the first to react. "It worked."

Podge seemed to be in a sort of trance. Eyes closed, he dropped to his knees, clutching his stomach. As he rolled onto his back, his jersey seemed to swell. A shape within began moving round, getting bigger and bigger until a split appeared in the material.

"C-call the police," stammered Psychic Sid. "I'm not arresting a bloomin' alien all by myself."

Two hands with black nail varnish on the fingernails were pushing their way out of Podge's jersey. Soon the

head and shoulders of Ms Wiz appeared. Carefully, she stepped out and brushed herself down.

"It's a nice place to visit, the underworld, but I wouldn't want to live there," she said.

Still lying on the floor, Podge slowly opened his eyes. "You wouldn't believe the dream I've just had," he murmured.

As Jack, Podge and Caroline ran to their parents, Psychic Sid squared his shoulders. "Ms Wiz, I'm arresting you for kidnapping three innocent children," he said.

"I don't think so." Ms Wiz walked forwards. When she reached the blackboard, there was a faint humming noise and she disappeared to be replaced by a small, neat drawing of herself on the board. "You'll be wanting my sister." Her voice sounded distantly from behind the blackboard.

"Huh," said Mr Harris. "She'll be another paranormal operative, I suppose."

"Oh no." The voice sounded fainter now. "She's an absolute, perfect . . . witch."

Jack smiled at Psychic Sid. "Would you like her address?" he asked.

THE SECRET LIFE
OF MS WIZ

Dear Reader

It is now several years since I first
received a visit from someone who
called herself Ms Wiz. She was a
rather unusual person, and she could
sometimes be quite annoying, but
down the years she has become a
very good friend of mine.

Now, something rather odd has
happened. Ms Wiz has asked me
whether, for the first and last time, she
could tell her own story. She said it
was all very well for me to sit here,
telling the world of all the things she
had done, and she wasn't
complaining (although, according to

her, my knowledge of magic is a bit dodgy, I should never have mentioned her age and I've written far too much about Herbert the rat).

But there are some stories, Ms Wiz told me, that are so strange and so private that only a true paranormal operative can tell them.

I am not a true paranormal operative. The fact is, I've never turned anyone into a warthog, my experience of time travel is extremely limited, and I make a mess of the simplest magic trick.

So it is time for me to step aside and let Ms Wiz tell you all about her secret life and the weirdest thing that has ever happened to her during her weird, weird lifetime.

Terence Blacker

Weird? My life? What on earth is he talking about?

No, the fact is that my writer has never quite understood me. I look much younger than he says I do, I'm quite a lot prettier, too. The pictures make my hair look spiky when in fact it has a gentle, natural curl to it, like a wave of dark loveliness. And I'm always in control of my magic – except when I'm not, which is very rare.

You, my readers, my public, deserve to hear the truth from the one who knows. So here, at last, it is.

Welcome to my own, personal, secret life.

Ms Wiz

Chapter One

Beagle Bad

If you are, or have ever been, a
paranormal operative, you will know
what it feels like when something
magical is about to happen. You feel
tense. Your head is woozy, as if you
have drifted off into a dream. From
deep within you, there is a low hum.
It gets louder and louder until people
all around you start noticing it.

Then, quite suddenly . . . BLAM!
All is peace and happiness and
loveliness. It's magic time again.

All these things happened to me,
Ms Wiz, on the day that changed my
life for ever. I was in the sitting room,
reading a story to my little boy,
William. He was wriggling around on

my lap like a dog with fleas.

There was tension. There was the wooziness in my head as if I had drifted off into a dream. A low humming noise was in the air. Normally I'm in control of these things but on this occasion something very odd was happening. I was not in control at all. The humming noise was coming from outside me. Someone else was causing the spell.

"Dolores!" At the very moment when I was beginning to wonder what exactly was going on, I heard the voice of my husband Brian. He was in the kitchen, doing the ironing. "Dolores, something rather unusual has landed in the garden."

"Unusual?" I said, without showing any particular interest. My husband is the kindest, sweetest man in the world but he tends to find

quite a lot of things unusual – the
colour of the tie worn by a TV
newscaster, for example, or the
amount of rainfall in one day, or
the way cornflakes go stale if you
don't seal them up properly.

"It seems to be a rather large white
bird," Brian was saying. "It's not a
seagull, so far as I can judge, and it's
definitely not a chicken. It may be an
owl but I'm almost certain that it's

an eagle."

The humming grew louder. William slipped off my lap and ran into the kitchen. "Beagle," he was shouting. "Me see beagle!"

I heard Brian correcting William in the quiet, careful way of his. "Not a beagle, little one. A beagle's a hunting dog. This is a great, white eagle."

A great white eagle? It could only mean one thing. Without a word, I stood up and scurried through the kitchen, past Brian and the Wiz Kid.

"What's that humming noise I can hear?" Brian called out. "I hope this isn't one of your spells. I've told you a thousand times. No magic. You are not Ms Wiz when you are in this house. You are Mrs Dolores Arnold."

I opened the back door. There, on the lawn, was an eagle of pure, dazzling white. Entirely unafraid, it began walking towards me. I smiled and opened my arms wide.

"Hello, Dad," I said.

As I spoke, the bird's feathers seemed to fluff out, then grow hazy, until there was no longer an eagle on the lawn but a swirling cloud of smoke, catching the rays of the sun.

"Did you say 'Dad'?" asked Brian, who was standing at the kitchen door, holding William's hand.

"Bad," said the Wiz Kid. "Beagle bad."

The cloud was beginning to take the shape of a person. A tall, elderly man, wearing a white suit and carrying a cane walking stick stepped through the smoke and walked towards me in a stiff, straight-backed way.

"Father." I hugged him gently and kissed him on both cheeks.

When I stepped back to look at him, he cleared his throat. "I am also your king."

I hesitated for a moment. The truth is, I've never been too happy with the whole kings and queens business. I believe that we are all equal and giving someone a special name does not make them better than you.

"Dolores?" My father smiled, as if he could tell what was going through my head.

I lowered my head and bent a knee in the quickest of curtsies. "Welcome, Your Majesty," I said.

"Excuse me," said Brian. "Would someone mind telling me exactly what is going on? Who is this man? Why did he arrive as a bird? And what is he doing on my lawn, pretending to be a king?"

My father held out his hand. "The

"Inappropriate? How can magic ever be inappropriate?" My father looked confused.

"Let's have a cup of tea inside," I said quickly.

It was not an easy tea party. William was showing off his latest spells, turning himself into a rabbit, flying around the room on a chair. Brian was becoming increasingly annoyed at this outbreak of magic. My father looked on, a polite smile on his face.

"Have you come far?" Brian asked at one point.

"From beyond the outer reaches of the known universe," said my father. "About a million miles beyond, I believe."

"That's a fair old hike," said Brian. "I have to travel in my line of business, too. These days, in the school inspection lark, you have to motor—"

My father clicked his fingers. In that instant, normal time was stopped. Brian sat as still and silent as a statue. William was immobile on his chair, a few inches from the ceiling.

"Sorry about that," said my father. "But we need to talk privately."

"Brian can be a bit . . . human sometimes," I said.

"He seems a nice enough chap." My father turned to me and fixed me with his piercing blue eyes. "I have decided that it is time for you to come home."

"But I am home."

"Home to your true home, the home of the blood, the family. The Palace of Wisdom needs you."

"Needs me?" I laughed nervously.

"What on earth for?"

"I'm tired, Dolores. After 10,000 years on the throne, I'm beginning to feel rather old. That is why I have decided that you, my daughter, should become the Queen of Wisdom."

"Queen?" My voice was a whisper. "I-I'm not sure about all that. What I believe is that we are all equal and giving someone a special name does not—"

My father interrupted me by clicking his fingers. Suddenly William was flying once more and Brian was talking again.

"It's the motorway travel that gets you," he said. "D'you find that, Arthur?"

My father's eyes were still fixed on mine. "Fortunately," he said, "I am about to retire."

CHAPTER TWO

Like . . . Forever?

After my father had left, I told Brian
that I needed to think. I walked out
of the little house that I had come to
love and down the High Street
towards St Barnabas School.

Home. The Kingdom of
Paranormal Magic and Utter Eternal
Mystery. Hardly a day passed without
my thinking about it. I missed
seeing my sisters and swapping spell
recipes with them and hearing all the
latest gossip from the paranormal
world.

On the other hand, there were my
friends from Class Five at St
Barnabas. As I walked towards the
school, I thought of all the

adventures I had been through with them. "I go wherever magic is needed," I had told them when I first met them in the days when they were younger and belonged to Class Three.

Since then, they had helped me as often as I had helped them. Every time when some little problem had occurred – like getting arrested by the police, or losing myself in history, or being turned into a doormat by my evil sister Barbara – my friends from St Barnabas had come to the rescue. Sometimes, to tell the truth, I felt that they were more grown-up than I am.

Still deep in thought, I approached the school gates just as the bell, marking the end of lessons for the day, began to ring. I noticed that some of the parents were waiting for their children so I stayed on the far side of the road. It was a bad time to be recognized.

I watched as some of my old friends – Carl, Nabila, Lizzie, Shelley Kelly – were greeted by their mums or dads and began to make their way home. Suddenly, it seemed to me that it had been a bad idea to come to St Barnabas; I turned and began walking away from the school.

"Yo! Ms Wiz!"

I heard a familiar voice and Jack Beddows appeared beside me, his hair dishevelled, and his shirt hanging out. The school bag slung over his shoulder looked as if it had just been used as a football.

Jack was beckoning across the road where I saw Caroline and Podge emerging through the gates. "It's Ms Wiz," he yelled.

Moments later, Caroline was

running across the zebra crossing, followed, more slowly, by Podge, whose mouth was full of chocolate, as usual.

"How are you doing, Ms Wiz?" Jack asked as we made our way towards the High Street.

"Not too terrible," I said.

Caroline peered up at me. "You look a bit worn out, if you don't mind my saying so," she said.

"Worn out? Me?" I laughed but the crack in my voice gave me away.

"What is it?" Podge asked. He looked at me quizzically. "What's happened?"

"I have some news," I said.

We sat, the four of us, side by side, on a park bench.

"Do you remember how you have

occasionally asked me where I come from?" I began.

"Yeah," said Jack. "And you always come up with the same totally annoying answer about telling us when the time is right."

"Now is that time," I said quietly. "The place where I come from is a strange place where nothing and no one are quite what they seem."

"Sounds like my house," said Jack.

"Its name is—" I hesitated, uncertain as to whether I should give away my secret "—The Kingdom of Paranormal Magic and Utter Eternal Mystery."

"Snappy name," Jack muttered.

"That is where the Wisdom family lives," I said. "There are twenty sisters. Most of us have been sent to different parts of the world to bring magical help to what we call 'normals'

– people like you."

Jack laughed. "That's the first time Podge has been called—"

"Now I have been summoned back," I interrupted. "My father has told me I must return to the Kingdom of Paranormal Magic and Utter Eternal Mystery with my little William."

For a moment, they looked at me in silence.

"Like . . . forever?" asked Podge.

I nodded my head.

"Can't you just say no?" asked Caroline.

"Yeah," said Jack. "No one tells Ms Wiz what to do. Not even her dad."

"He's not just my dad," I said. "He also happens to be the king."

"The *king*?" All three of them spoke at once.

"But, Ms Wiz, you don't believe in

the monarchy," said Caroline. "You've always said that we are all equal and giving someone a special name does not make them better than you."

"I know I said that," I agreed. "That's why I never mentioned to you that I'm a princess. It didn't seem important."

"You, a princess? Now you *are* kidding us," said Jack.

I shook my head. "My precise title is Her Royal Highness Princess Dolores of the Kingdom of Paranormal Magic and Utter Eternal Mystery."

Jack seemed to find this rather funny. "No wonder you call yourself Ms Wiz," he said.

"And now," I said miserably, "my dad wants me to be queen."

"Wow!" said Podge. "Queen Wiz."

"It's terrible," I said. "I'll have to boss people around and make sure they treat me with respect and spend all my life using my incredible power to make sure that everybody's doing things that please me. And that's just not like me, is it?"

For some reason, the children were staring at their shoes. "No, Ms Wiz," said Caroline eventually. "That really doesn't sound like you at all."

"I don't know how you're going to manage it," said Podge, who seemed to be trying to keep a straight face. "You've never bossed anyone around in your life."

Suddenly I felt my eyes pricking with tears. "The trouble is I like it here. I love seeing you all and having adventures. I'm even getting used to your jokes."

The four of us sat staring gloomily

across the park for a few moments.

Jack clicked his fingers as if he had just had a brilliant idea. "You go back to your land of utter amazing whatever and you tell it straight to your dad that no way is old Muggins here going to be queen. You say to him, 'If you want to retire, kingy – you get one of the other sisters to do it'."

I lowered my head. "I wouldn't

dare," I said quietly.

"Not even if your mates from Class Five were there to back you up?" asked Caroline.

"Nice one, Caro," said Jack. "We could tell the king that we're not going to let you go."

I looked at them and smiled. "You'd have to step outside time," I said. "We'd need to travel a million miles beyond the outer reaches of the known universe. You would be the only normals in the Kingdom of Paranormal Magic and Utter Eternal Mystery."

"And," said Podge, "where, exactly, is the problem?"

I smiled. "Do any of you get travel sickness?" I asked.

One after another they shook their heads.

"Close your eyes and hold on very tightly to the bench," I said, as the humming noise grew louder. "It is about to take you farther than any normal has travelled before."

"Will we be back in time for tea?" asked Podge. "I'm starv—"

And we were gone.

CHAPTER THREE

Going Native

The old home looked the same. When
we opened our eyes, our park bench
was on a long green lawn. The sun
was shining gently and the sound of
birdsong was in the air. Ahead of us,
surrounded by trees, was a big,
rambling old house with roses
climbing up the front. From inside
could be heard the laughter of
children.

"This is my home," I said. "What
d'you think?

Podge, Caroline and Jack stood
looking at it for a moment.

"It's not what I imagined," said
Podge, eventually. "I was expecting a
big old castle on the edge of a cliff

with eagles flying between the spooky towers."

"It's just a house," said Jack. "A very old house."

Caroline seemed to be waking from a dream. "Well, I think it's lovely," she said walking towards the steps which led up to the front door. "It may not look weird or magic, but it's perfect."

"It's up to the ruler of the kingdom to decide what the Palace of Wisdom should look like. In the past it's been a castle, a rabbit burrow and a tropical island. My father's a traditional type. He likes it like this."

Jack was looking around him. "So, where's the Kingdom of Utter Eternity?" he asked. "All I can see are trees and fields and stuff."

"The kingdom is all around us and also within us," I said. "We take our eternal mystery wherever we go. We are together and yet alone. We are here, now, and yet we are also the past and the future. We are all masters and yet we are all servants."

"What, even when you're queen?" asked Jack.

I thought for a moment before correcting myself. "We are all masters and yet all of us, except one, are servants."

I opened the front door. In the Great Hall, two of the children could be seen flying from one beam to another. One of my uncles was in a big leather chair, sipping a cup of fire. The piano was playing "Nelly the Elephant", all by itself. A group of rats were chatting in a corner. It was as if I had never been away.

"This is such a strange place," Podge murmured.

"All homes are strange in their own way," I said.

"Except most of them don't have talking rats, self-playing pianos, fire-eaters and flying children," observed Caroline.

No one had seemed to notice us, so I walked through the hall, followed by Jack, Podge and Caroline. When we reached a great oak door at the end, I knocked firmly three times and entered.

My father was behind his desk. His eyes were closed and his head was resting sideways on the wing of a high-backed chair.

"Behold the king upon his throne," I said softly.

"Where are all his pages and foot-servants and courtiers?" Caroline whispered.

"In the Kingdom of Paranormal

Magic and Utter Eternal Mystery, we don't need them." I approached the desk and said, "Father."

His eyes opened slowly. When he saw that I was there, he sat up sharply. "Yes, that's right, do that," he barked, and straightened up in the chair. "Ah, Dolores, I've just been doing some work."

"In your dreams," muttered Podge.

"Exactly, dreamwork can be extraordinarily useful, I find." For the first time, my father noticed that I was not alone.

"Who are these young people?" he asked.

"Your Majesty, this is Jack Beddows, Caroline Thompson and Peter Harris, who prefers to be called Podge."

"Welcome to you all," said the king.

"Bow to the king," I muttered out

of the corner of my mouth.

"You what?" said Jack.

There was nothing for it. I took a
deep breath and the humming noise
was all around us. As if a great
invisible hand had thwacked them
on their backs, the three of them fell
forward on their faces.

"Please, please." My father laughed
modestly. "There is absolutely no
need to abase yourselves before me.

I'm only a king, after all. What very nicely brought-up children you are."

"Yes, aren't we," grumbled Caroline as she stood up and dusted herself down.

"I shall assign them magical duties this afternoon," said my father. "Which spells are your specialities, my dears?"

"We don't exactly do magic," said Jack.

"Don't do magic?" The king looked surprised. "How very odd."

"They're—" I hesitated, concerned how my father would take the news. "Well, actually, they're normals, Father."

"Normals?" The king looked slightly surprised. "Oh well, I'm sure they'll learn soon enough. Welcome to the Kingdom of Paranormal Magic and Utter Eternal Mystery. I'm sure you'll be very happy here."

There was an awkward silence.

"Actually—" It was Jack who spoke.
"We're only visiting."

"We have families to get back to,"
said Caroline.

"And food," said Podge. "It's
teatime."

"Father, I'm just here briefly," I
said. "I need to discuss something
with you." I turned to Jack, Caroline
and Podge. "Would you like to
explore the house?"

They looked uncertain.

"Or would you prefer to stay here,
frozen in time?"

"Let's go," said Jack.

"Your Majesty, I have a problem," I
said a few moments later when I was
alone with my father. I took a deep

breath. "The fact is, I'm happy where I am."

He smiled. "Of course you are. And we're very happy to see you, too."

"I mean that I'm happy there – with the normals, looking after little William, being with my husband Brian."

"William can come with you and Brian can visit any time he wants."

"Then there's Class Five at St Barnabas School."

My father frowned. "And what exactly has Class Five at St Barnabas School got to offer which cannot be found in the Kingdom of Paranormal Magic and Utter Eternal Mystery?"

I sat down in seat in front of his desk and spoke about some of the things I had done with Class Five. I told him about Herbert running up the school inspector's trousers, about the time I turned everyone in the Houses of Parliament into monkeys, about when I became a doctor and a head teacher and the occasion when I ended up reading the news on television. I talked about becoming a supermodel, going back in time, falling in love with the most famous film star in Hollywood, Brad Le Touquet. I even revealed that my evil twin sister had captured Podge, taken him deep into the underworld and turned him into a zombie slave.

"That Barbara." My father chuckled. "She always was a bit flighty."

"What I'm trying to say is that I'd miss all that," I said. "I don't think I'm quite ready to be queen."

"You've gone native, that's your problem. I've seen it many times

before. Often when a paranormal
operative spends too much time
among normals, she starts wanting to
be normal herself."

"Maybe someone else could be
queen for a while. One of the other
sisters or—" I hesitated "—Mother."

The king looked away quickly as if
he had noticed something terribly
interesting in the garden outside the

window. "Your mother appears to find the continent of Africa more interesting than her husband," he said quietly. "I have not seen her for over a year."

I sighed. "So there's no one else, then?"

My father squared his shoulders. "I am your king and this is my command," he said. "Go to the

Operations Room. Visit some of your sisters and talk to them about this. I shall need a decision from you by the end of today."

I stood up, gave a quick curtsey and made for the door. "Thanks, Dad," I called out over my shoulder.

CHAPTER FOUR

Dumped Big-Time by the Frothies

There was no time to lose, but when I emerged from my father's study there was no sign of Jack, Caroline or Podge. As soon as I started looking for them through the house, aunts and uncles noticed me and wanted to chat while children pestered me for new spells.

Some of the rats scampered after me, asking for the latest news of Herbert. Eventually, to shut them up, I told them about his marrying a street-rat called Arabella and that they had thirty-two children. "Probably thirty-six by now," I added. "I haven't seen him for a couple of hours."

Leaving the rats muttering among themselves about this news, I went outside. There, on the croquet lawn, some of the children of the palace were teaching Jack how to fly, laughing as he spread his arms and made his first nervous flights.

"Spells are for later," I said briskly. "We have to fly around the world in the next few hours."

As I spoke, Jack landed in a crumpled heap on the grass. "Around the world?" he said. "I can only just get off the ground."

But I was on my way back to the house. "Follow me," I said.

"She's behaving like she's queen already," muttered Caroline.

I took them through the hall. Under the stairs was a heavy metal door against which I placed my hand. It opened slowly and we descended the forty-nine steps to the Operations Room.

It was a small circular room with screens on every wall. "This is the nerve centre of the kingdom," I said. "From here, we can track what every paranormal operative is doing."

I pressed a button near the door. The lights lowered and all the screens lit up.

"Wow!" said Jack. "It's the ultimate telly room. Can we watch *The Simpsons*?"

"You are now surrounded by my family," I said. "In the next few hours, we have to find which of my sisters could be queen instead of me."

"Can we get a takeaway pizza while we watch?" asked Podge. "My stomach's begging for mercy."

Caroline was looking from screen to screen. "They're all doing different things and they all look exactly like you," she said.

"Isn't it a bit embarrassing being watched all the time?" asked Jack. "What about when you want to be private – like when you go to the toilet?"

"Grow up, Jack," said Caroline. "Paranormal operatives don't go to the toilet."

"Maybe they have magic, invisible loos," said Jack. "And when they—"

"Stop it, stop it, stop it!" I shouted. "Here we are, facing the biggest moment in my entire life as a paranormal operative and all you can talk about is . . . ablutions." I turned to one of the screens where Ludmilla Wizgova could be seen climbing a mountain with a group of normals. "I don't think she's suitable to be queen somehow."

"Do we just talk to them through the screen?" asked Podge.

"No, we visit them. One tap on the screen and we'll be transported to whichever part of the world they are in. The only question is, who to visit? We only have time to see three of them."

I looked at one screen after another. My family certainly seemed to be

having a good time out there.

"Hey, surfing," Jack called out from
the other side of the room. "Take a
look at that—" He reached out
towards the screen.

"Jack! Look out!" I shouted.

But it was too late. There was a
muffled explosion and a blinding
flash of flame. When we were able to
open our eyes again, the only sign of
Jack in the Operations Room was a

small plume of smoke.

I glanced at the screen where he had been standing. Across some golden sands, I saw my sister Ms Wazza walking beside a tall, broad-shouldered man in torn-off jeans who had a surfboard under his arm. Running behind them was Jack Beddows.

I sighed. I had a few moments to find a new queen for the Kingdom of Paranormal Magic and Utter Eternal Mystery and Jack had transported himself to the other side of the world. "It looks like our first trip is to Australia," I said.

"Australia!" Caroline clapped her hands. "Can we see where they make *Neighbours*? Will there be kangaroos? And koalas? I love koalas."

"Will we back in time for tea?" asked Podge.

"Give me your hands," I said. I touched the screen, there was a flash and suddenly we were sitting on a beach, blinking at the brightness of the sun.

"And a very g'day to you, mates," said my sister Ms Wazza. "Nice of you to fly in."

I stood up, brushing the sand off my jeans. "Hullo, Scarlett," I said, kissing her on her tanned cheek. "These are my friends Caroline, Podge and Jack."

"Hi," she said. "Welcome to Byron Bay, choicest spot in the wide brown. This is my mate Clyde. We're looking for the perfect wave. We caught an absolute beaut up the coast but we're getting dumped big-time by the frothies on this stretch, y'know?"

Jack, Caroline and Podge looked confused. Scarlett frowned. "Don't these kids speak English, Sis?" she asked.

"Yes, but it's slightly different English from yours," I said. "I was under the impression that you were in Australia for magical purposes."

Scarlett laughed. "Good old Dolly." She winked at Clyde. "She always was the goody-two-shoes of the family." She turned back to me. "I did a few spells back in town. Now I'm chilling out with my mates, trying to use some magic to hold up a wave so that it carries me right across Byron Bay."

"That sounds great," said Jack. "Could I have a go?"

Clyde dropped his surfboard on to the sand. "No worries, I'll give the kid a few lessons on dry land and then—"

"I think not," I said briskly. I drew

241

a double circle in the sand around Jack, Caroline and Podge. "We're off back to the Operations Room."

"But Ms Wiz—" Jack began to protest, but I held up a hand and stepped into the circle.

"Nice to meet you, Clyde," I said. "And Scarlett, if I were you, I'd put in a bit of paranormal work down here, otherwise you might get sent somewhere else in the world." I smiled coldly. "I've heard that Siberia's free."

"No drama," Scarlett muttered. "I might get back to town to cast a spell or two right now."

I whispered, "Operations . . . " and by the time, I had added " . . . Room," we were back home.

Caroline looked around her. "All right, Ms Wiz. I have to admit it – I'm dead impressed."

I shrugged. "Travelling around the world's easy when you know how," I said.

"Not the travelling," said Caroline. "It was the way you took hold of the situation. Scarlett really looked up to you."

"Between you and me, I don't think she was queen material," said Jack.

I looked around the screens. "Well spotted, Jack," I said. "But who is?"

"How about this one?" asked Caroline. "She seems to be in charge of some sort of circus."

"Not a bad idea," I said. "Her name's Ms 用 邪 法 个 女 人."

"Er, 用 邪 法 个 女 人?" said Jack.

I moved towards the screen. "You can call her Wiz Phu, for short."

CHAPTER FIVE

Hello Dolly

We were in a gigantic circus tent. High above our heads, a girl was doing some exercises on a tightrope. A family of jugglers were throwing swords to one another while, on the other side of the circus ring, two clowns were going through a custard-pie routine.

In the centre of the ring stood a woman in riding gear, carrying a whip which she was cracking now and then. It was my sister, Wiz Phu, and she was bossing people around, as usual.

"No, no, no! You're falling before the pie hits you," she was shouting at the clowns. "Try it again."

"Wiz Phu?" I spoke gently.

Wiz Phu glanced towards me. "Hey, welcome, Sister. Good to see you," she said, as if we ran into each other every day of the week. "Step out of the ring, will you? I won't be more than an hour."

I stood my ground. "We haven't got an hour," I said. "I need to talk to you about something very important."

Wiz Phu laughed angrily. "Something more important than the *Wiz Phu Circus of Magic and Mystery* which happens to be playing in Beijing next Monday? Somehow I'd be surprised." She looked at Caroline, Jack and Podge. "Who are these children?" she barked. "Have they got permits? Strangers are banned from the rehearsal area."

Caroline moved closer to me. "Your

sister's dead scary," she murmured.

"Come to think of it, you kids can make yourselves useful," said Wiz Phu. "Tell me if you think this is funny." She screamed at the clowns, who were standing, dripping with custard, to carry on. One of them picked up another pie. Holding it high in the air, he walked towards the other clown. Just as he approached, he tripped. Custard flew everywhere.

"Well?" Wiz Phu glowered at the children. "Was that funny? Did it really make you laugh?"

"Yeah, ha ha," said Jack, straight-faced. "It . . . cracked me up."

"I almost split my sides," said Caroline nervously.

"What about you?" Wiz Phu asked Podge.

"I was wondering if you had any spare custard pies," he said. "It was

such a great act I'd like to practise
at home."

Wiz Phu seemed to relax and
turned to me. "What was it you
wanted to ask me, Dolly?"

I was tracing a double circle in the
sand around myself, Jack, Caroline
and Podge. I smiled at my sister.
"Nothing," I said quietly. "I've
changed my mind."

Back in the Operations Room, the four
of us gazed at the screens around us.

"Boy, am I glad St Barnabas got
you," Jack said eventually. "Your
sisters are all nutters. Ms Wazza just
thought about herself and Wiz Phu
was like the most power-crazed
teacher there's ever been."

"You were so good with them."
Caroline smiled at me. "I reckon

they're lucky to have someone like you as a sister."

I walked slowly around the screens. As I looked at my nineteen sisters, I realized that, much as I loved them, not one of them was going to be able to take charge of the Kingdom of Paranormal Magic and Utter Eternal Mystery. On the last screen, I watched an older woman. She was sitting under a big shady tree, surrounded by little African children.

"It's our last chance," I said. "You are about to meet my mother."

I held out my hand towards the screen.

"Well, hello, Dolly!"

The face that I loved, but had not seen for a long time, looked up from the book she was reading and smiled as if she had been expecting me. "Come over and join us under the baobab tree."

The four of us picked our way through the children. I kissed Mother and introduced her to Caroline, Podge and Jack. She stood up and addressed her class. "This is my daughter and her friends," she said. "Her name is Ms Wiz. So, what do you say to her?"

"Good morning, Ms Wiz," the class

said in unison.

"Now I know she would love to tell us all about her life," said my mother, "because she's a teacher, too. Only she does her paranormal magic in a faraway land."

I smiled. "I promise I'll come back to talk to you," I told the African children. "But right now I've got to have a quick talk with my mum."

Mother handed out picture books to her class and told them to read to themselves under a nearby tree. When they had settled down, she said, "Well, what would you like to do while you're here? See around the village? Watch the animals at the waterhole?"

"There's no time, Mum," I said. "I've come to talk to you about Dad."

My mother sighed. "I suppose he's as busy as ever, running his blessed kingdom."

"He misses you," I said.

"And I miss him. But I had to come out here to do this for myself. All I used to be was the king's wife. Now I'm being myself. I'm putting magic to good use."

"He wants to retire, Mum. He thinks it's time someone else took over."

My mother clapped her hands, almost as if she were a little girl. "That's wonderful news. He'll have more time to spend with me. If I came back, we could be just Mr and Mrs Wisdom again." She closed her eyes. "No more running the kingdom morning, noon and night. What bliss that would be."

I hesitated and, in that moment, I knew that I had been wrong to think that my mother could be queen. She needed a rest as well. It was time for her to be a grandmother. "I know he'd really like that, too," I said.

"And that was what you came to tell me? That Dad wants me to come back? How sweet of you, dear."

By now Jack, Caroline and Podge were staring at me. I knew that they understood why I had changed my mind.

"Yes," I said. "That's why I came. I'll tell Dad you'll be back as soon as you've said goodbye to your class."

I stood up and carefully drew a double circle in the earth.

"There was one other thing, Dolly." My mother was frowning. "If your father is descending from the throne, who is going to take over from him?"

"Oh, didn't I tell you?" I smiled. "I am."

CHAPTER SIX

Prince Brian

We travelled through time and space but now our destination was not the Kingdom of Paranormal Magic and Utter Eternal Mystery. The two circles that I had traced around us when we were under a baobab tree in Africa took us home to a park bench in St Barnabas Park.

Jack scratched his head. "Er, Ms Wiz," he said, "was that a dream or have we just been to the Kingdom of Magical Utterly Utterness, met your dad, who happens to be king, popped over to Australia and then China before seeing your mum in Africa?"

"Dream? Reality? Magic? Truth?" I smiled. "What, at the end of the day, do they all mean?"

"At the end of the day, it's the end of the day and that means it's past my teatime," grumbled Podge. "If we stepped out of time, how come I'm getting hungrier all the time?"

"Paranormal magic has great power," I explained. "But there are some things that are too powerful for it to control – the weather, life and death, mighty earthquakes, the tides

of the oceans. And the appetite of Podge Harris. Your stomach is a force of Nature."

I noticed for the first time that Caroline was staring sadly across the park. "It wasn't a dream, was it, Ms Wiz?" she said quietly. "You've decided to become queen."

"Not queen exactly," I said. "I believe that we are all equal and that giving someone a special name does not make them better than you. I'll probably call myself something simple and humble like 'Her Royal Highness'."

"HRH Ms Wiz," said Jack. "I've heard it all now."

"That means you'll be leaving," said Caroline. "You'll be so busy running your kingdom that you won't have time for a little class from St Barnabas."

I put my arm around her. "One of the great things about being a royal highness is that I can do exactly what I like," I said. "So I can come and visit you now and then. I can even invite you back to the Palace of Wisdom if you feel like stepping out of time again."

"I'll make sure I bring my lunch box next time," muttered Podge.

I stood up. "It's time for us to go back to our families," I said. "I have one last favour to ask of you. I'd like all my friends to gather in the school playground at noon tomorrow – children, parents, teachers, even PC Boote."

"How can we arrange that?" asked Caroline.

I smiled. "Class Five can do anything it sets its mind to," I said.

"There could be a fire alarm," said

Jack. "And the parents could have been summoned to see Mr Gilbert. And an emergency call just might have been put through to PC Boote at the police station. These things could just happen."

"We'd better get going," said Caroline more cheerfully. "We've got some calls to make."

The three of them stood in front of me. "I'll see you tomorrow at noon," I said. "Thanks for helping me make up my mind. I don't know how I'm going to reign without you." I kissed them quickly, one after the other.

"We'll be there whenever some Class Five magic is needed," said Caroline.

I laughed. I watched them as they made their way out of the park. At the gate, they turned and each of them waved once more. It was time to go

back to the house. I needed to talk to
Herbert, and then to Brian.

"Sorry, old bean. Not a chance. I
wouldn't dream of moving."

Herbert was sitting on his chair as
four of his children scrambled all
over him. He held in his paws a
picture book called *Ratman* which he
was trying to read to them. On the
carpet nearby, lying on her side, his
wife Arabella was feeding five babies.
Their other twenty or so children
were playing rat games elsewhere
in the room, running up curtains,
nibbling the edge of the carpet and
playing hide-and-seek in the chest of
drawers.

"The Palace of Wisdom is our true
home," I said. "You may like it here
but you're a magic rat. You belong in

the land of magic."

Herbert raised his little arm as if he were a policeman holding up the traffic. "Speak to the paw. The head ain't listening," he said. "Now, where were we, children?" He returned to his book and started reading, "Is it a bird? Is it a plane? No, it's Ratman!"

"The choice is yours, Herbert," I said. "You either come home and spend your life chatting with the other rats and doing spells. Or you stay here and become an ordinary street rat – rummaging around dustbins and living in a sewer."

Herbert gave a little shudder. "I don't think dustbins and sewers are quite me somehow," he said.

At that moment, Arabella looked up and gave him a wide, yellow-toothed smile.

"But what about my other half?"

Herbert asked, dropping his voice as if Arabella could understand what he was saying. "She wouldn't exactly be at home with all that magic. She's a rat normal. She can't even talk."

"I can sort that out," I said. "I'll give her a voice. I am going to be queen after all."

"Hmm." Herbert pondered for a moment. "But what will she be like when she can talk? I mean, between you and me, she might be . . . well, you know, NQOCD – not quite our class, darling."

I was going to tell Herbert that it didn't matter how people spoke, that it was what they said that mattered, when I had a better idea. Humming filled the room, and Arabella started as if suddenly awakening from a deep, deep sleep. She looked up at Herbert.

"What is that *ghaaastly* book you're reading, darling?" Arabella's voice was high-pitched and squeaky, like a chalk on blackboard. "I always hoped our little ones would learn to read by looking at *Vogue*. Taste and manners are *sooo* important in the young."

I winced. There had been no way of telling what Arabella would be like when she had a voice. It turned out that she was an even bigger snob than her husband.

But, to my relief, Herbert was smiling as he put aside his copy of *Ratman*. "Darling, I've just had the most marvellous idea," he said. "How would you like to move house?"

Leaving Herbert and Arabella to make plans for their new life, I made

my way downstairs.

Brian was in the kitchen, feeding William who was in his high chair. I kissed them both, carefully avoiding the food around the Wiz Kid's mouth, and sat at the table, watching them for a moment, my husband and my little boy.

"I've been to see my father," I said.

"Arthur?" said Brian. "How was

he? Still flying around as a bird, pretending to be a king?"

"Sort of," I said. "D'you remember I told you that he was going to retire?"

Brian nodded. "I do seem to recall something of that nature," he said.

"Well." I took a deep breath. "King Arthur told me that he would like me to be supreme ruler of the

Kingdom of Paranormal Magic and Utter Eternal Mystery."

Brian spooned another helping into William's mouth. "That would be quite a promotion," he said eventually. "What a shame you can't accept."

When I said nothing, he looked up sharply. "You can't accept, Dolores, can you?"

"I have to go home," I said quietly. "William needs to be among magical children like himself. It's his destiny."

"And what about my destiny?"

"You could come too. You would be Prince Consort to me – Prince Brian."

Brian laid the spoon down. William waved his arms. The spoon lifted off the plate, dipped into the food,

hovered upwards and carefully fed
him.

"I don't want to be a prince," he
said, almost as if he were talking to
himself. "I like being a school
inspector. I have lots of work to do
here."

As William fed himself, I spoke
about my journey home. I told Brian
how I had travelled around the world

with Jack, Caroline and Podge. I
spoke about my father and my
mother. Like the Wiz Kid, I too had
my destiny to fulfil.

When I had finished, Brian thought
for a moment. "You took those
children from Class Five with you?"
he asked. "And they didn't have to
become paranormal
operatives?"

I shook my head. "Jack had a go at
flying but basically they were the
same as ever. We just stepped out of
time. When we came back, it was as
if we had never been away."

"I see."

"You could do that, too." I spoke
softly. "You could be prince consort
one day, school inspector the next.
You would have two homes, and two
lives for the price of one."

Brian gazed out of the window.

When he looked back at me, he was smiling. "Now *that* sounds like a bargain," he said.

CHAPTER SEVEN

The Rat Carriage

Why is there always a fuss whenever
I decide to do something? There was
a fuss when I arrived at St Barnabas
and did some magic, as if turning
teachers into farmyard animals was
somehow "unnatural". There was a
fuss among the paranormal
operatives when I fell in love with
Dracula and decided to marry him.
There were other fusses when I
became Prime Minister, visited the
underworld and lost a couple of
classes when I was head teacher.

But now there was the biggest fuss
of all.

Back in the Kingdom of Paranormal
Magic and Eternal Mystery, when I

returned to my father's study, I found my parents sitting together, holding hands.

"Thanks to you," my father smiled happily, "my dear wife has returned from Africa. Now all that I need to complete my contentment is to see you crowned as the new queen."

And that was where the fuss began. I told my father that I would be honoured to become the new ruler but that I would have a coronation without a crown or dressing-up or parades with massed brass bands or angels flying over the palace in "V" formation or being brought to the throne in a giant rat carriage or having the children dressed up in velvet and lace or any of that usual royal stuff.

"What is more, Father," I said, "I shall not allow myself to be called the queen. I shall simply be HRH

Ms Wiz."

The king seemed to sink in his chair. "Oh, Dolores." He buried his face in his hands. "Why do you always have to be different?"

"I'm not different. That's exactly the point. What I believe is that we are all equal and that giving someone a special name does not make them better than you."

"But you *are* different, Dolly," my mother said in her most reasonable voice. "You're the supreme ruler."

"And if that's the case," I countered, "I'd like everything in the kingdom to be modern and fair-minded."

"But the people at the palace like a bit of a show now and then," said my father. "It's the old Wisdom tradition. In many ways, paranormals are very normal."

"Well, it's time they grew up," I said firmly. "All this bowing and scraping is old-fashioned and downright embarrassing. It is time for the spirit of change to reach the kingdom, for old Wisdom to make way for new Wiz."

My father squared his shoulders and gazed seriously into my eyes. "I am your father," he said. "I am also your king. This is my decree."

For the first time in thousands of years, I stared back at the king and refused to bow my head. "Well, Dad," I said quietly, "put it this way. It's new Wiz or no Wiz."

There was a moment of tense silence. Then, to my surprise, my father began to laugh quietly. "You're going to be quite a queen," he said.

"HRH."

He nodded his head, still smiling. "Quite an HRH," he said.

So we agreed to meet each other halfway on the question of the coronation.

The ceremony would take place in the Glade of Majesty, deep in the woods, as is traditional. I agreed that the mighty host of paranormal operatives could be present as usual but instead of being dressed in gold and silver with traditional peacock and raven feather accessories, the dress code would be "smart casual". I refused to wear the crown – a ridiculous, towering thing of priceless jewels which would make my neck ache – but agreed to accept a simple diamond tiara. The brass band would be there but, instead of playing the aggressive marching tunes that were traditional on these occasions, they would play a medley of Abba hits. There would be a fly-past but, rather than being restricted to angels, anyone from the kingdom who fancied a bit of a fly could join in.

There was something of a problem with the rat carriage. In the past, the rats of the palace joined paws and generally tangled up together in a very complicated and beautiful way to make a royal carriage, which would bear the future monarch across the lawn to the Glade of Majesty. When I told the rats that I thought that the sight of a person, even an HRH, lying back in a carriage made out of their own bodies was an insult to rodent dignity, they told me that they had been rehearsing for this day for years.

In the end, I agreed that the carriage would proceed as usual but on one condition – Herbert and Arabella would sit with me to show that, during the reign of HRH Ms Wiz, rats and paranormal operatives would live as equals.

As for the ceremony itself, I insisted on new Wiz wording. The king was reluctant to agree, some of the sisters threatened not to show up, but, in the end, I calmed their fears. I told them that, in the Kingdom of Paranormal Magic and Utter Eternal Mystery, we had always believed in change – after all, our magic was changing things all the time. Now it was time for us to change, too.

And there was something else that I did – something so unusual that I could tell absolutely no one about it. The day before the coronation, I flew once around the forest glade, spreading sand as I went. Then I flew around once more, tracing two lines in the sand.

At this great moment, the coronation of their new HRH, the people of the Kingdom of Paranormal Magic and Utter Eternal Mystery would be in for a surprise.

CHAPTER EIGHT

Dancing Queen

The sun was shining on the day that I would become the ruler of all that is magic and paranormal. A hum of excitement hung over the woods surrounding the palace as crowds gathered for the coronation.

At a few moments after eleven o'clock, the procession emerged from the gates of the palace courtyard. Behind the flag-bearer stood my father, smiling at my mother by his side. They moved towards the lawn, followed by my sisters who walked two by two except for Barbara, who stood alone at the back, a look of thunderous jealousy on her face. Then came the band, followed by aunts and uncles of the Wisdom family and special guests from the palace.

Finally, in a majestic carriage of writhing rats whose dark coats seemed to glisten in the morning sun, came me, HRH Ms Wiz. On my right was Herbert, wearing a natty purple waistcoat and spotted bow tie. Beyond him was Arabella, who waved graciously to the crowd as if she were really the one that everyone had come to see. On my left, babbling happily, was William, soon to become Prince Wiz Kid.

We made our way past the palace entrance and the croquet lawn and up the great avenue of trees which leads to the Glade of Majesty. Here the procession halted. As is the tradition, my father was the first to step into the glade. He walked

towards the ancient oak that stands at
its centre. A throne has been carved
out of its trunk, on each side of which
the tree's branches spread like
mighty green wings. My father
ascended the steps of the oak throne
and took his seat.

"I am Arthur," he announced.
"This morning, I am King Wisdom,
Master of Magic, Sire of Spells, Peer
Extraordinaire and Supreme

Sovereign of the Kingdom of
Paranormal Magic and Utter Eternal
Mystery. On the stroke of midday, I
shall be king no more but merely
Arthur Wisdom, citizen. From that
moment, your ruler shall be—" The
king paused and turned his eyes to
me. "Your ruler shall be Dolores, my
beloved daughter."

From the woods all around us,

there was the sound of applause like rain falling on leaves. I alighted from the rat carriage and made my way into the glade, followed by Herbert, Arabella, William, my sisters, aunts and uncles and the members of the palace court.

At this moment of my crowning glory I stood before the throne, my head bowed, my heart thumping with fear and excitement. From the palace behind us, the first chimes of the great clock could be heard. My father stood up, took the three steps downwards and placed the simple tiara on my bowed head. He then kissed me gently on the cheek, and with his hand under my elbow, guided me to the first step. On the sixth chime, he released me. I mounted the steps and turned.

The clock chimed eight, nine, ten . . .

From the forest around us, a low humming noise could be heard. It grew louder and louder.

. . . eleven, twelve.

I raised my hands. The forest was engulfed in a heavy mist. It cleared slowly. The glade was no longer surrounded by trees. The crowd in the woods could no longer be heard. The oak throne, the Glade of Majesty and all who stood in it were in a new place altogether, in a school playground.

"Wow, what a tree house!" shouted a voice that I recognized.

"Its not a tree house." I smiled down on Jack Beddows. "This happens to be my oak throne."

"It's Ms Wiz!" shouted Lizzie. There were cheers from Class Five.

For a few seconds, I enjoyed the strangeness. Close to me, in the

Glade of Majesty, were William, my
mother and father, my sisters,
Herbert and Arabella. Then beyond,
just outside the magic circle, were the
people, the normals, with whom I had
done so much. At the front of the
crowd, I saw Jack, Podge, Lizzie,
Caroline, Nabila, Carl, Kelly and all
the other children of Class Five.
Behind them I saw the school staff –
Mr Gilbert, the head teacher, Mr
Bailey, Miss Gomaz, Mrs Hicks – and,
with them, the librarian, Mr Goff, the
local policeman, PC Boote, and some
of the parents.

Standing slightly apart from the
other adults was my own sweet
school inspector husband, Mr Brian
Arnold.

I turned to the court before me.

"I, HRH Ms Wiz do solemnly
declare—" Before I could go any

further, I was aware of a kerfuffle in the crowd. Mr Gilbert burst into the Glade of Majesty, followed by Mrs Hicks and Miss Gomaz, with PC Boote bringing up the rear.

"You can stop that right now," said the head teacher, puffing slightly. "While we are always happy to see old friends at St Barnabas, it is strictly against school regulations for strangers to enter school premises without written permission."

"Strangers?" I smiled. "These are not strangers. They are my family, the royal dynasty of the Kingdom of Paranormal Magic and Utter Eternal Mystery. This is the crowning of the Mistress of Magic, Dame of Spells, Peer Extraordinaire and Supreme Sovereign of the Kingdom."

"Just listen to her. She thinks she's so special," muttered Mrs Hicks.

"Talk about giving yourself airs," said Miss Gomaz.

PC Boote stepped forward. "There is absolutely no way that tree is legal," he said. "It constitutes a serious safety hazard to the kiddies in this playground."

"But this is my coronation," I protested. "It only happens once every 10,000 years or so. I thought you'd be pleased that I decided to hold it at St Barnabas."

"Regulations are regulations," said PC Boote firmly.

I smiled down from my throne. In the past, my spells had turned teachers into geese and sheep, and once I had turned the staff of an entire police station into rabbits, but this was my special day and I was in a good mood. As a distant humming noise could be heard in the playground, I put a love spell on them.

Suddenly, Mr Gilbert seemed to forget all about me. He turned to Miss Gomaz. "Why, Miss Gomaz, you're . . . beautiful," he said, blinking up at the teacher.

Mrs Hicks had grabbed PC Boote's hand. "You know I've always found

men in uniforms fearfully attractive," she said.

"Oh, please, Ms Wiz," Podge shouted from the front row. "This could get seriously embarrassing."

I raised my hands once more. Silence descended on the crowd.

"I, HRH Ms Wiz, do solemnly declare—" I glanced across at Class Five. "I solemnly swear that I am not going to change one bit," I said. "I have always said that I would go wherever magic is needed. Right now, magic is needed in my own kingdom and that is where I shall be."

There were mutterings of disappointment from the class.

"But—" I paused for a moment. "All my friends from St Barnabas will be welcome to visit me at any time. My beloved husband Brian Arnold will be moving from one world to the other. All you need to do is contact him."

There were cheers from Class Five.

Brian smiled up at me and it was at that moment that a low rumbling hum seemed to fill the air. The oak throne where I was sitting rose slightly off the ground and soon the entire Glade of Majesty, with my family, Herbert and Arabella, seemed to hover in the air above the playground. Behind me, the band struck up with my favourite Abba song "Dancing Queen".

.Above the noise, I noticed that Podge seemed to be shouting something. He pointed desperately at Mr Gilbert and Miss Gomaz, who were still in each others' arms. Beyond them PC Boote was walking hand in hand with Mrs Hicks towards the school gates.

"Whoops." I remembered the love spell. Smiling, I pointed to Mr Gilbert and Miss Gomaz. They sprang apart, as if suddenly realizing what they were doing. Mrs Hicks stood back from PC Boote, arms crossed. They were once again the way they used to be. Everyone at St Barnabas was the same as I had always known them.

We were getting fainter now and, to my surprise, I noticed that my eyes had filled with tears. I gazed downwards at Class Five and, through the blur, they smiled up at me from the playground as if they were a single, friendly face.

I waved my hand and slowly, slowly, they began to fade from sight.

The Wiz Kid was crawling up the steps of the oak throne. I picked him up and held him to me.

At last, the time had come – we were going home.

THE AMAZING ADVENTURES OF MS WIZ

Terence Blacker

Join the world's most famous paranormal operative on three of her most hilarious magical adventures!

TIME FLIES FOR MS WIZ

POWER-CRAZY MS WIZ

MS WIZ LOVES DRACULA

MS WIZ MAGIC

Terence Blacker

Three fantastically funny stories
about the magical Ms Wiz!

IN CONTROL, MS WIZ?

MS WIZ GOES LIVE

MS WIZ BANNED

A selected list of titles available from Macmillan Children's Books

The prices shown below are correct at the time of going to press. However, Macmillan Publishers reserves the right to show new retail prices on covers, which may differ from those previously advertised.

Also by **Terence Blacker**:

The Amazing Adventures of Ms Wiz	ISBN-13: 978-0-330-42040-2 ISBN-10: 0-330-42040-2	£4.99
Ms Wiz Magic	ISBN-13: 978-0-330-42039-6 ISBN-10: 0-330-42039-9	£4.99
The Crazy World of Ms Wiz	ISBN-13: 978-0-33043136-1 ISBN-10: 0-330-43136-6	£4.99
Ms Wiz Superstar	ISBN-13: 978-0-330-43406-5 ISBN-10: 0-330-43406-3	£4.99

All Pan Macmillan titles can be ordered from our website, www.panmacmillan.com, or from your local bookshop and are also available by post from:

Bookpost, PO Box 29, Douglas, Isle of Man IM99 1BQ
Credit cards accepted. For details:
Telephone: 01624 677237
Fax: 01624 670923
Email: bookshop@enterprise.net
www.bookpost.co.uk

Free postage and packing in the United Kingdom